The School Factory

Christine A. Adams

COPYRIGHT

THE SCHOOL FACTORY:

Second Edition- Reprint

Copyright©2025 Christine A. Adams

Published by Hanley-Adams Publishing – 2025

Print ISBN 13:   979-8-9992651-0-4

eBook ISBN 13: 979-8-9992651-1-1

CreateSpace

Charleston, SC

First Edition

Copyright © 2010 Christine A. Adams

Cover Design: Marcia Firsick

Middlebury, CT

ISBN: 1449560555

ISBN-13: 9781449560553

The names and identifying details of the case histories, and narrated portions, found in this book have been changed. Any resemblance to persons living or dead is coincidental.

DEDICATION

To all my former students for all they taught me about life, love and the beauty of innocence.

THE SCHOOL FACTORY

by

Christine A. Adams

The End

On June 10th Heritage High School will graduate 130 seniors. The Graduation means the end of production on the assembly line at The School Factory. Mrs. Anderson, the senior English teacher, is involved in an accident on Kick Hill road as she hurries to the graduation. In her unconscious state time shifts and she returns to events of the school year, she remembers certain students and incidents:

THE JOURNEY *from September 10th --- June 10th The morning of the first day of school, all of her classes from the lowest level English to Advanced Placement - A Parent's Night, The Spirit Assembly, The Band Rehearsal, the Funeral, The PPT Meeting, and Partying At The Sand Pit, to the immediate events of June 10th - Graduation Day.*

THE STUDENT PRODUCTS IN THE SCHOOL FACTORY

1. <u>Larry Blaisdell</u> - the boy who can't read but is a firefighter. On the night of graduation, be rescues Mrs. Anderson from her car just before it bursts into flames.

2. <u>Josh Spenser</u> - a remarkable, inspirational young man who was born with Cerebral Palsy. He overcomes his disability to become an Olympic athlete.

3. <u>Eric Berman</u> - an exceptional **AP** student, Editor-in Chief of the Yearbook, an athlete, and The Valedictorian.

4. <u>Leslie Schroeder</u> - Eric's girlfriend - a beautiful, artistic girl who lives with a single mother. She will go to Rhode Island School of Design while he goes to Brown.

5. <u>Latisha Emmons</u>, the only African American girl in the senior class, who is also the most talented and most intelligent girl. Her attendance falls off in the spring and she doesn't make Valedictorian.

6. <u>Frank Sargent</u>, whose step-mother molested him, lives in a shack behind the Abbott farm. He obsesses about girls and sex and wanders aimlessly around town when he's not •working the farm.

7. <u>Sylvia Smith</u>, who lives next door to the farm, befriends Frank and he warns her about her wild friends. After z concert in Ludlow, when Sylvia drank and used ecstasy, she received a head injury in a car crash. She never could regain her short-term memory even when Mrs. Anderson tutored her.

8. <u>Suzy Stevenson</u>-a teen mom.

9. And <u>Justin Tobin</u>-two seniors who have a two-year old kid named Billy. Their parents are feuding. Mrs. Anderson intervenes.

10. <u>Jim Bartlett,</u> a very talented musician, a gay boy who is plagued by a homophobic father and permissive mother. After being "outed" by his friend, he commits suicide.

11. <u>Alex Brady,</u> an **ADHD** special needs student is really an alcoholic who is in the last stages of alcohol and drug addiction. He hates school and spends most of his time playing in a band. He is confronted by Mrs. Anderson at a PPT meeting and gets help.

12. <u>Ryan Blakely</u> - a spoiled rich kid had been expelled from a private school because he blew up a stink bomb in the boys' bathroom. His parents paid tuition to transfer him to Heritage High. At Heritage, he took up "pushing drugs and pills." By the end of the year he is in serious trouble!

In her unconscious state, Mrs. Anderson hears the sonorous, overbearing **VOICE OF EDUCATION** *that constantly intrudes into her mental space with educational jargon about ----- -*

- PRODUCTS ON THE ASSEMBLY LINE

- ACCOUNTABILITY EDUCATION - NO CHILD LEFT BEHIND

- SPECIAL NEEDS PROGRAM - THE RESOURCE ROOM

- PARENTAL INVOLVEMENT

- THE SCHOOL BUDGET - KEEP TAXES FROM GOING UP?

- PRODUCTS THAT REPRODUCE PRODUCTS

- SPIRIT WEEK- INTENDED TO "LIFT THE SPIRITS" OF THE PRODUCTS

- EXCESSIVE ABSENTEEISM- HOW TO KEEP TRACK OF THE PRODUCTS

- DEFECTIVE PRODUCTS- SOME PRODUCTS DO NOT FUNCTION

- TUITIONING SOME STUDENTS TO DEFRAY COSTS

Time finally shifts to the graduation ceremony itself. By this time, Mrs. Anderson has been transferred from **Kick Hill Road** to a Life Star helicopter. She loses her battle for life just as the copter flies over the ceremony. Her spirit leaves her body - The spirit of her student, Jim Bartlett, joins her and they observe the graduation below.

They see Larry arriving late; they see the memorial musical tribute to Jim himself. They see the kids getting their scholarships and diplomas. When the hats are tossed, two hats float skyward - one belonged to Larry who tried to save Mrs. Anderson and the other to Kurt, Jim's friend. Mysteriously, they are snatched up with the wind. Jim reaches into the future to show Mrs. A. how some of the kids live out their lives.

Thus, the day ends at The Beginning.

THE END IN THE PRESENT
JUNE 10*TH* - GRADUATION DAY

Graduation day is an ending day!

Mrs. A., as her students called her, was running late. 6 o'clock! It starts at 6:30 she thought. Quickly, she slipped a white silk dress over her head and maneuvered a gold chain out from under it. As she zipped the back of the dress, her feet struggled to get into last year's pumps there on the floor. She wiggled her toes in place and grabbed her small white purse from the bureau.

"I can't be late," she said as she pulled the front door shut. The Mazda Miata seemed to have heard her and swung into action as she pulled away from her house on Thorndike Road.

No one to wave goodbye to. No one to wait there for her to come home. Jenny Anderson in her 18th year as a teacher at Heritage High, was divorced with a son in college and a recent "empty nester."

She hated that label because she knew its hidden pain. Now, with her son at Brown University, she concentrated on her "kids at Heritage." She couldn't be late for their graduation.

She hit the accelerator on Kick Hill Road and raced the engine. The old lady in the Oldsmobile in front of her was too deaf to hear her and too blind to see her.

"I have to see them march in," Jenny exclaimed as she drove her palm into the steering wheel. "Com'on lady."

Every year on graduation day it was the same. She was happy for her students but sad at the same time. That made the day almost impossible to bear. Last year, she went back into the school to pick up some books and cried as she walked the empty corridors. Because she was a teacher of "seniors", her loss was always inevitable and immediate.

In a way she felt the school was like a factory. The kids like products that get pushed along the assembly line. Every year different names, different faces, but somehow the same kids. She thought of this year's class, Josh, Eric, Leslie, Suzy, Justin, Larry and Alex. She hoped she didn't cry when she saw Josh lumber up to the podium or when Eric gave his Valedictory speech - but she probably would.

Distracted for a moment she forgot the old lady in front of her until she noticed the clock at 6:10. Impatient, she decided to take a chance and pass the old lady on **Kick Hill Road**. Impulsively, she pulled out around her.

At that moment, Jenny saw the square bumper of a truck bearing down towards her. The bumper was high off the ground; the body of the red truck had white letters on it. She didn't have time to look at the driver, or the name on the truck, just the big black square bumper. She knew the truck was going to hit her. The driver seemed not to be a person but a flurry of activity someplace up high in the air. Hemmed between the Oldsmobile and the oncoming truck, there was no time or space to get out of the way.

The blow of the collision drove her back into the seat as the steering wheel cut into her chest. She felt the blow – the car moving backwards, the airbag swallowing her, and then she knew only blackness.

Someplace in that blackness the structure of time was

erased. Time shifted and Jenny was getting ready for the first day of school – this year, last September, this graduating senior class.

THE PAST JOURNEY

SEPTEMBER 10TH – THE MORNING OF THE FIRST DAY OF SCHOOL

6 AM - To make that initial impression on the seniors at Heritage High and to make sure her feet didn't hurt by the end of the day, she put on the new red plaid dress with the comfortable black flat shoes.

As she dressed, Jenny Anderson, a petite 42 year old veteran teacher who had always loved the excitement of teaching, mentally ran through the lesson plans. Two British Literature Level One classes early in the day – give out books, explain the course outline. Assign notes Anglo- Saxon period. Advanced Placement period 4 – Start reading in the Sequel Book. Explain concepts of Literary Criticism. Hand out Dostoevsky's Crime and Punishment – 50 pages by Wednesday. Late in the day, English Level Two – have them start notes in class. Then, last period of the day English Level Three – Introduce course, start notes, and show film to introduce Anglo Saxon period.

On the way to the School, Mrs. Anderson thought of her students wondering what the year would bring. A school bus stopped in front of her. She hit the brakes and waited. "It's almost like a factory, a school factory," she said out loud. "The number of kids, the same problems and they get passed along like some manufactured products – no time – just 'keep movin' kids."

As she turned into the parking lot, she thought of that funny scene on the Lucy show when Lucy and Ethel were working in a candy factory and struggling with the moving assembly line. She remembered when they were stuffing candy into their faces, and into their pockets but they couldn't catch up. The line kept moving faster and faster. She laughed.

"Hey, Ms. A. I'm back." She looked up to see Larry Blaisdell knocking on her car window.

"Hey, Larry, what's happening?"

Larry's was the kid who quit last year. A really good kid, but a really bad student! She was glad he was back "to graduate this time." She also knew Larry couldn't read past the fourth grade level and needed intensive daily tutoring taking him back to that level and bringing him up to grade level. It would never happen she thought – no time, no resources!

Larry and Ms. A. joined the stream of students making their way into the building as Mrs. Anderson silently worried if Larry would make it this year.

BACK ON KICK HILL ROAD

The 9-11 call came from a cell phone. "There's been a terrible accident." We need an ambulance on Kick Hill Road. Right past Emmett's Garage. A woman in her forties – she's unconscious. Hurry."

Right after the impact, Jenny shifted in and out of consciousness. A heavy darkness hung over her mind like a shield protecting her from some unexplainable, horrific pain. Time stood still as that darkness was interrupted. She thought she heard a chorus of voices but then heard only one loud sonorous male voice called "EDUCATION." It talked to her in a terrible monotone that made her sleepy but even though it hurt her ears she knew she had to listen. It said:

"HERE ARE YOUR PRODUCTS! YOUR **SCHOOL FACTORY** IS ON A HILL. IT RISES UP FULL OF HOPES AND DREAMS CALLED **THE FUTURE**. SOME CLAIM IT IS **THE AMERICAN DREAM.**

IN THE FACTORY, THERE ARE SEVERAL LONG CONVEYOR BELTS THAT TRACK THE PRODUCTS. WE START OFF WITH THE GROUP CALLED **THE SUPER INTELLIGENT**, OR GIFTED; THEN, COMES **THE INTELLIGENT**; AND FINALLY, **THE AVERAGE** AND **BELOW AVERAGE.**

IF YOU WORK AS A **TEACHER** AT THE FACTORY FOR ABOUT TEN YEARS, YOU MIGHT BE ABLE TO MOVE FROM THE AVERAGE ASSEMBLY LINE TO THE INTELLIGENT. IF YOU ARE GIFTED YOURSELF, YOU MIGHT BE ABLE TO WORK WITH THE SUPER INTELLIGENT. EACH YEAR, **THE DEPARTMENT HEAD** GIVES OUT **EVALUATIONS** AND **ASSIGNMENTS** – A GOOD EVALUATION MIGHT MEAN AN ASSIGNMENT TO A HIGHER LEVEL.

HERE'S HOW IT WORKS! ALL THE PRODUCTS ARE PROPELLED ALONG ON THEIR **TRACK** EACH DAY. THE SUPER INTELLIGENT, OR GIFTED, HAVE A SPECIAL **EDUCATIONAL PROGRAM** AND THEIR BELT GOES FASTER THAN ALL THE OTHERS, PLUS THEY HAVE MORE BOOKS AND TEACHERS.

IT COSTS MORE TO MOVE THEM ALONG.

ADVANCED PLACEMENT KIDS CAN READ AND WRITE EXTREMELY WELL AND WILL PROBABLY DO WELL ON THE **ADVANCED PLACEMENT TEST** THAT IS GIVEN AT THE END OF THE LINE. THERE IS A CHANCE OF THEM BEING MOVED ALONG TO THE **IVY LEAGUE COLLEGE** CHUTE IF THEY CAN REACH A SCORE OF 5. THE LOCAL NEWSPAPER WILL PROBABLY PUBLISH THEIR SCORES AND NAME THEIR COLLEGES.

THE **GIFTED** PRODUCTS ARE ALWAYS SHINED AND PRESENTED TO THE PUBLIC AS MERCHANDISE THAT IS TYPICAL OF THIS SCHOOL FACTORY. MOST OF THE TIME THE KIDS ON THE OTHER CONVEYOR BELTS, ESPECIALLY THE BELOW AVERAGE AND SPECIAL NEEDS LINE, ARE USUALLY NOT ASKED TO CONDUCT AN ASSEMBLY, ACT IN A PLAY, OR WRITE FOR THE SCHOOL NEWSPAPER.

THE PRODUCTS ON THE REGULAR INTELLIGENCE LINE ARE GENERALLY WELL EDUCATED WITH REGULAR BOOKS AND REGULAR TEACHERS. SOMETIMES THEY HAVE APPRENTICES, OR **STUDENT TEACHERS**, TO HELP MOVE THESE CLASSES ALONG THE LINE. THEY CAN READ AND WRITE WELL AND WILL PROBABLY GO TO THE **LOCAL UNIVERSITY** OR **COMMUNITY COLLEGES**.

THE PRODUCTS ON THE AVERAGE CONVEYOR BELT WILL BE GIVEN BOOKS THAT LOOK ALMOST LIKE THE BOOKS OF THE INTELLIGENT PRODUCTS BUT THEY WILL NOT BE

THE SAME – NOT QUITE AS HARD. THERE WILL BE HOMEWORK BUT NOT AS MUCH AND NOT ALL THE TIME. THEY WILL BE ABLE TO READ AND WRITE ALMOST AS WELL AS THE INTELLIGENT PRODUCTS AND THEIR PAPERS WILL BE GRADED WITH A'S AND B'S. BUT THE A'S AND B'S WON'T MEAN THE SAME THING AS THE A'S AND B'S ON THE OTHER BELTS BECAUSE THE **GRADES** ARE **WEIGHTED.**

WHEN THE AVERAGE PRODUCTS COME TO THE END OF THE LINE THEY WILL PROBABLY GO TO ONE OF THREE CHUTES – **COLLEGE, MILITARY SERVICE** OR **EMPLOYMENT**."

BACK ON KICK HILL ROAD

Somewhere in the darkness Jenny Anderson sensed a loss. She slipped even deeper into her darkness as the red stain on her white dress grew larger. She thought she heard someone say "Larry, Over Here!! Over here!!" and then she heard Larry Blaisdell's booming voice. "Let's get her out of here. It's going to blow. I smell gas. It's going to blow!" Then, she felt her body being scooped up, amidst an unending pain that threw her back into school, her most dreaded class Period 6, Level Three, - Larry Blaisdell's class.

THE PAST JOURNEY
SEPTEMBER 10ᵗʰ – THE LAST CLASS ON THE FIRST DAY OF SCHOOL – PERIOD 6 - LEVEL THREE - ENGLISH

Mrs. A. looked at the clock 12:55. Time for her last class of the day and it was the hardest one to handle. This was the lowest division and most kids in the class couldn't read very well. They hated English and just wanted to graduate. Usually they tried to distract the teacher and the class with humor or hostility - just so they didn't have to do the reading and writing they hated so much. You couldn't expect homework to be done because it would take hours to do it.

Larry, an imposing six footer who weighed well over 200 pounds, made his entrance into Room 02 as the last bell rang. His aqua and orange plaid shirt barely covered his round chubby arms; but somehow the shirt worked with his fiery red hair and huge grin. You couldn't hate Larry because everyone knew he just hated school. No one took it personally. Larry had a rough time in the first grade and missed out because a young teacher tried to teach reading with sight rather than sound. None of it made any sense to Larry and he missed the whole thing.

Soon he fell behind and couldn't read with any speed at all. Last year it got so bad he quit school but decided this year to come back and finish. The worst days of his life were days when he had to read out loud. No one at home knew how to help him so Larry fell off the education conveyer belt early and could never get back on.

This first day of school, Larry flopped into the third seat in the row near the windows and cranked open the window near him as he sat down.

"Larry, don't open the friggin window!" came from the kid in the fourth seat. No response. So the kid in the first seat got up and cranked the window shut.

Suzanne, who sat across from Larry, figured it would take these guys ten minutes to settle down," Can I go to the Ladies Room?" Every day it was the Ladies room or The Nurse's Office for Suzanne. Her distraction was to leave the room to get away from Larry.

"No, Suzanne, not now!"

Marcy got up from her seat at the back of the room and walked carefully down Larry's aisle to the pencil sharpener. There is something about Marcy's walk – a kind of floating on air walk – that walk was never lost on the boys in row one. Whrr, whrr, whrr, the pencil sharpened. She returned to her seat knowing she had the full attention of all the guys in the room.

Larry never brought a pencil to class and if you could get him to write a paper in class and asked him to re- write it for homework, the paper would somehow disappear in his truck. If you asked him to read a chapter in a book, he would say he forgot or didn't have time because he had to work. The Blaisdell family owned one of the largest pig farms in Vermont. Larry worked the farm every day.

Mrs. A looks at the clock – 1:05 – ten minutes into the class and nothing done yet. The distractions are working!

"Alright, class, settle down." she said, emphatically, as she handed a pencil to Larry. "Turn to the first section of your literature book - the Anglo Saxon History – take notes from pages 2- 8. We'll see a short film at the end of the period." Reluctantly, the kids open their books. Mrs. A circulates the room helping some of them get started.

In the middle of the film, Larry's beeper went off and he bolted from the room. One of the kids whispered to Mrs.

Anderson, "Volunteer - Emergency – Ambulance. He needs to go! He's got permission!"

"I know, I know." This was the second year Mrs. Anderson had Larry for English so she knew about his beeper. The class resettled itself with big Larry gone.

LARRY – THE FIRST PRODUCT

Larry wasn't much of a success in school but in his life outside of school, he was very successful. The Blaisdell Hog Farm was a thriving business. One of the largest in the state.

All the four sons worked the farm. They all lived over on the east side of Heritage. There was Chet, who lived across the street from the farm with his wife, Linda, and their two kids. He went to school for accounting so he handles the money. Mason Blaisdell just got married last summer to Sally Reider who was a local girl from town. They moved into the old Newick homestead out on Parson's Way. Mason handles the selling of the pigs. Larry and Porter are still at home working the farm. Seems like the father had a bad spell last year and doesn't do much physical work anymore. He just buys more land for his boys.

Running the pig farm isn't all Larry does in his spare time. He can't read but he can fight fires and drive the rescue truck and ambulance. Whenever there is trouble in town, like the fire at Emmett's house at 2 AM, the accident out on Rt. 21, and the day the kid fell into Long Sought For Pond, Larry is there to help. He's become a kind of local hero by pulling people from twisted car wrecks, saving kids from drowning, and even rescuing Mrs. Moulton's cat from the oak tree in her yard. Around town Larry is known for his fiery red hair, his boisterous good nature but also for his compassion. No one who was in trouble ever asked him if he could read.

BACK ON KICK HILL ROAD

In the darkness, Jenny Anderson sensed an internal struggle. The Voice of Education kept saying, BUT HE CAN'T READ! Then another more Powerful Political Voice chimed in and said, "THE SCHOOL AND THE TEACHERS SHOULD BE ACCOUNTABLE BECAUSE NO STUDENT SHOULD GRADUATE UNTIL HE CAN READ."

Then an even more Powerful Legislative Voice said, "WE WILL MAKE THE SCHOOLS TEST LARRY AND IF HE DOESN'T PASS, HE WON'T GRADUATE."

Mrs. A. tried to yell out, "This is wrong! This is wrong!" But no one heard her! The voices became louder:

WHAT ABOUT **ACCOUNTABILITY?** WE HAVE STUDENTS WHO ARE GRADUATING HIGH SCHOOL WHO CAN'T READ! WE WILL PASS LEGISTLATION CALLED **"NO CHILD LEFT BEHIND"**. EACH SCHOOL WILL TEST THEIR PRODUCTS TWICE A YEAR TO PROVE **ADEQUATE YEARLY PROGRESS.** SCHOOLS WHO HAVE LOW TEST SCORES FOR TWO YEARS WILL BECOME **"SCHOOLS IN NEED OF IMPROVEMENT"** THEY WILL GET **LESS FEDERAL ASSISTANCE.**

IF THEIR PRODUCTS CAN NOT REACH HIGHER PROFECIENCY LIVELS IN **READING AND MATH** IN FIVE YEARS, ALL THE TEACHERS

WILL BE DISMISSED AND THE SCHOOL WILL BE TURNED OVER TO THE STATE.

EDUCATORS OBJECTED SAYING, "INSTEAD OF MAKING MORE PRODUCTS 'PROFICIENT IN READING AND MATH' THIS LAW WILL MAKE THINGS WORSE. **THE MOST PROFECIENT KIDS** WILL PASS THE TEST AND TAKE IT EASY FOR THE REST OF THE YEAR: **THE MIDDLE PROFECIENCY GROUP** WILL JUST BREATHE A SIGH OF RELIEF AND TAKE IT EASY FOR THE REST OF THE YEAR: AND **THE ALMOST PROFECIENT BUT NOT QUITE** KIDS WILL GET THE MOST HELP FROM THE TEACHERS IN THE HOPES THEY BECOME PROFECIENT AND PASS THE TEST.**THE HOPELESSLY LOW PROFECIENCY KIDS, LIKE LARRY, WILL SIMPLY BE ABANDONNED."**

EVEN THOUGH A HUGE PERCENTAGE OF SCHOOLS FAILED, THE PRESIDENT AND THE POLITIANS COULDN'T ADMIT DEFEAT SO THEY YELLED EVEN LOUDER ABOUT **THEIR EDUCATIONAL REFORM.**

IN THE PRESENT

JUNE 10ᴛʜ - GRADUATION DAY AT 6:20 PM LARRY GETS THE CALL FOR HELP

Larry was running late to graduation. He had just finished his chores, showered and shaved. Checked his beeper for messages. Nothing. When he got in his truck, he saw the time.

"I need to get mov' in," he said   Then, remembering his graduation cap and gown, he bounced out of his truck and ran back to the house. His mother was standing at the door with the blue robe over her arm. She knew her son was forgetful and didn't want to show her irritation - after all he was willing to go <u>back</u> to graduate. It's never been easy for Larry she thought.

"We'll be right along. Don't want to miss <u>this</u> day." Mrs. Blaisdell watched as her son sped out of the driveway. The Police scanner in his room had been crackling but she turned it off. "Not tonight" she said to the machine that usually dominated her son's life.

But in Larry's truck, his beeper went off. The dispatcher said there was a serious accident over on **Kick Hill Road**. A sports car and a truck!

"Jesus, I got to go. This's gonna be a bad one — especially with a truck — and on Kick Hill Road." Larry whipped his truck around and swung into the fire station. He made it just in time to hop on the emergency truck. The fire engine roared out behind him.

BACK ON KICK HILL ROAD

When Larry saw the red Mazda Miata he knew it was Mrs. A. He grabbed a neck collar from the truck, ran to where her life-less body was buried in the air bag, instinctively reached in to check her carotid for a pulse.

"She's alive." he yelled to Jed, the driver of the rescue truck. The volunteer ambulance screamed off in the distance.

A trickle of smoke emerged from the engine. "Smells like gas, Larry!" Jed said as he backed away from the car. No time thought Larry. Have to get her out. Instantly, Larry attached the neck brace, pulled opened the mangled door cutting his hand as he ripped it open, and carefully lifted her out to a safe place on the grassy knoll beside Kick Hill Road. The truck driver was already sitting there dazed and shocked.

The instant Larry laid her down, Mrs. A's much admired sports car exploded in a fiery ball. As Linda Pierson, also one of Mrs. Anderson's former students, was pulling up in the ambulance, she saw the sports car on fire, but she didn't recognize it. She did know if anyone was in that car no medical help would be needed that day. Larry Blaisdell was yelling and then gestured wildly to Linda to move in front of the exploding car.

"My God, that's Larry Blaisdell and he's pulled another one out of a wreck." Larry was yelling something about his teacher. "Has he gone crazy?" She jumped down from the ambulance and ran to the grassy knoll.

Instinctively, when Linda saw the red stain spreading out on the white dress, she applied pressure to abate the bleeding. "We'll need special help here. We need more help! She has special needs. Alert Life Star!"

"We'll get her in the ambulance and out to that clearing," Larry said as he made contact with Life Star.

As Jenny Anderson lay on the grassy knoll, she felt a pressure in her chest and in her head. She understood they needed more help for the special needs kids. How could they successfully include them in every class? She felt confused. But THE VOICE of EDUCATION took over her mind and shouted to be heard:

"WE HAVE A **SPECIAL NEEDS PROGRAM** IN OUR SCHOOL. WE CAN TAKE CARE OF OUR **SPECIAL NEEDS KIDS**! EVER SINCE THE STATE PASSED THE **DISABILITY ACT**, THE SCHOOL HAS PRACTICED **INCLUSION** IN EDUCATION. SOME KIDS WITH SEVERE PHYSICAL AND MENTAL DISABILITIES HAVE JOINED THE MAIN STREAM.

ON THE MAIN FLOOR OF THE SCHOOL FACTORY,THE GIFTED, WITH THE REGULAR INTELLIGENCE, AND AVERAGE INTELLIGENCE ARE TRACKED ON LONG COMNVEYOR BELTS THAT END IN CHUTES MARKED COLLEGE, MILITARY, OR EMPLOYMENT.

THE **COURSE WORK** THAT THESE KIDS LEARN IS TAILORED TO THE CHUTE THEY ARE DESTINED FOR. LIKE FIRST YEAR COLLEGE COURSE STUDENTS TAKE HIGHER MATH - ALGEBRA I & II SO THAT THEY CAN TAKE GEOMETRY AND CALCULUS LATER. THE NON-COLLEGE COURSE STUDENTS TAKE MATH I OR MATH II SO THAT THEY CAN TAKE BUSINESS MATH.

STUDENTS THAT CAN'T DO EITHER OF THESE COURSE CURRICULUMS ARE SOMETIMES DEEMED BELOW AVERAGE STUDENTS WITH SPECIAL NEEDS. THEY ARE TAUGHT BY SPECIAL NEEDS TEACHERS IN THE **RESOURCE ROOM**.

OUR RESOURCE ROOM IS IN A DIFFERENT BUILDING AT THE BACK OF THE FACTORY – A **SPECIAL NEEDS** AREA. THERE ARE ONLY A FEW

KIDS ON EACH BELT AND IT GOES VERY SLOW. THE TEACHER HAS SEVERAL APPRENTICES TO HELP THESE PRODUCTS TO READ AND WRITE. EACH KID WEARS A SIGN, OR LABEL – SOME HAVE INITIALS THAT STAND FOR **DEFICIENCY, DISABILITY** OR **DISORDER** OR **DISEASE** – ALL DIFERENT CONFUSING LETTERS.

WHEN THESE PRODUCTS GET OUT INTO THE HALL FOR LUNCH THEY TRY TO HIDE THESE LABELS BUT ONCE A LABEL IS STUCK ON THEM YOU CAN SEE THE IMPRINT AND THE OTHER KIDS KNOW THEY ARE THE SPECIAL NEEDS LINE FROM THE BACK OF THE BUILDING."

BACK AT KICK HILL ROAD

On the gurney, in the ambulance, Mrs. A. felt the pressure on her throat as they checked her carotid artery. Linda, noted her shallow breathing and set her up for oxygen. Jenny regained consciousness long enough to realized that her body felt disabled. She couldn't move. Her body was heavy and it wouldn't work right. So, this is a dis - ability? Cerebral Palsy – like Josh. Time split in two and darkness melted into light as Jenny returned once again to September 10th and the first class of the day, Josh's class.

THE PAST JOURNEY
SEPTEEMBER 10th – THE FIRST CLASS ON THE FIRST DAY OF SCHOOL – PERIOD 1 LEVEL ONE - ENGLISH

Ms. A. grabbed a cup of coffee in the teacher's room and made her way to Room 02. Confidently she walked to her desk, deliberately looking out into the class to catch her first look at the level one class and to let them know she was a veteran and not afraid of what they had to dish out this year.

Just as the last bell rang, the door opened and Josh kind of flopped in. He made his entrance by dropping his books on the floor as he fumbled to shut the door.

"SSS S orrr y," he said with a smile that negated the twisted voice of his cerebral palsy. The kids who didn't know Josh laughed and the kids who did helped him pick up his books. Josh had been removed from the lower level classes to Level One classes when it was discovered that he was an extremely bright, avid reader who could compensate for his inability to write by taking oral tests and writing on the computer.

"OK, let's begin. Let's go over the course outline." The fifty-six minute period quickly folded into twenty-six minutes. When Mrs. A could see Jake's eyes shutting, she knew that the class had heard enough about British Literature.

"Welcome to your senior year!" Jake's head nodded as he heard her words. "OK, this little exercise might help you when you get to your college essays." Again, Jake snapped to attention. The clock hummed its unusually loud hum and Betsy stopped doodling on her notebook.

Mrs. A. explained that everyone has a special talent – a talent that has to be defined. Usually, colleges ask you to write about yourself and your special talents. She explained this as she handed, to the first person in each row, a paper with four questions on it. She motioned them to pass it back. They did.

Benjamin had taken out a math book and was starting the first exercise in the book. Quickly, Mrs. A closed his book, "Only English in this room." Jake seized the moment and borrowed a pencil from Ben. The questions on the paper read:

1. What did you love to do as a child?

2. Who do you think you are?

3. What do you love? What could you do that you know you would absolutely not fail at it?

4. What is stopping you from pursuing your dreams?

As the pencils scratched on the paper, Jake wrote about sports and his concern about getting picked for the college draft; Betsy talked about her love of art, her dream of getting into Art School, and her concern that her portfolio would be accepted. Ben recognized his ongoing love of math and science and hoped to be accepted in an engineering program. Jean talked about her writing and how she'd like to major in English. Justin and Jenny showed their answers to each other.

Josh laboriously scribbled his answers on his paper bearing down so hard that he almost ripped the paper. His letters were very big and his shaky hands made lines that were squiggly instead of straight. His answers were mostly one-word illegible strangulated shapes. Mrs. Anderson wondered how Josh would be able to handle this level one class.

Finally, just before the bell and after the sports, art, and engineering she said, "So what do you have, Josh? What did you love to do as a child?"

"Ww- inn- tter Ss- kee-ing!" came with a smile from the twisted body of Josh. The room grew quiet; the clock hummed louder.

"Who do you think you are?"

"Bb- ussiness – pro- profess- ional m-man."

"What do you do the best? What do you <u>know</u> you absolutely could not fail at?"

"Ss-kee-ing Hh-elp pp-eoople."

"What is stopping you from pursuing your goal?"

"Not-tt-hing!" His smile widened as the bell rang and the kids stacked their papers on the teacher's desk. Jake proudly nudged Josh as he passed by his seat. Josh teetered unsteadily as he acknowledged the nudge and seesawed out the door into the hall.

JOSH – THE SECOND PRODUCT

Josh was born with cerebral palsy and was not MAIN STREAMED until he was 14. Our factory was supposed to process him through to GRADUATION because of the DISABILITY ACT that the LEGLISLATURE passed stating that all children with disabilities had to be included in the regular public schools. Once again, in 2004, the Senate renewed this act.

The first time he passed Jenny Anderson in the hall she was shocked. The effort it took for him to walk was astounding. His arms were like heavy tree limbs swinging wildly in a wind storm. His head moved aimlessly with his jerky body and he seemed to push his whole body forward with the force of a hurricane. Yet, even with all that physical difficulty there was something wonderful about Josh – his attitude, his spirit.

Because Josh was only a freshman and she taught seniors, their paths didn't cross often but every time she saw him, she felt the presence of his powerful, optimistic spirit. When he spoke, it was as if he had gravel down in his voice box. Sometimes the halting sounds were very long and very harsh but he never failed to speak.

During his junior year, the senior class was invited to a special assembly that Josh had set up. It was an assembly to promote understanding about disabilities. Josh had organized it, promoted, and brought in outside speakers from the State Disabilities Board, and a doctor to explain how cerebral palsy happens. The class was astonished and moved by his opening words, "I aam Jossh Sspenn-serr aand I haave Cereebrrall Pallssy. MYY Dis Dis Abb il it y H-happennd when I wass born." He went on to tell the kids more about himself and his disability.

When Josh was four years old, his parents were told that he'd probably never walk. Nevertheless, Josh kept trying; he walked. Then Josh wanted to learn to ski. Time after time, he fell but eventually he skied. Oh, how he skied! By the time Josh came into Mrs. A's class as a senior, he had become a downhill racer. He attained his Alpine Competitor License and won the Eastern Cup in Alpine racing for two consecutive years. In addition to racing in The National Handicapped Ski Tour, he became a member of the United States Olympic Handicapped Ski Team.

Josh told the press, "Wh-een you put-t your mind to ssom-ett- hing, you can do-o it. I ddo-n't car-re what others te-ell you."

As part of his senior project, he spent time speaking to middle school students about the Special Olympic World Games. During one presentation to a seventh grade class, Josh talked about his experiences traveling with the Olympic Ski Team. He said, "I'm dis-sabbled, but I'm an athlee-te first. Ww-hen I make my rr-un, my mm-ind says 'athlee-te, athlee-te'."

Josh told Mrs. Anderson that when he started talking to the younger kids that they were tentative when he first started to speak. "Thee-y ww-armed up to m-me. Tth-en, tt-ten studd-ents asked mm-e for my autt-to-graph," he added laughing.

Everyone at the School factory became his fan too. The school nurse said, "Nothing stops him, he's not afraid of anything." The secretary in the office said, "He's a role model for a lot of kids. He enlightens them."

Once when asked what a person should do when they meet a disabled person, he said, "Thh-e moo-st important thh-*ing is thh-at we-rre people first and diss-abb-led second. A-and we never gg-ive up.*"

IN THE PRESENT
JUNE 10ᵗʰ - GRADUATION DAY – EARLY AFTERNOON - 2:30 PM - JAKE AND HARRY DEFEND JOSH

Josh's mother asked to leave work early on June 10ᵗʰ. She would pick up Josh at school to take him for a haircut. Josh had been refused a driver's license when he was sixteen. That was the worst day for him.

His mother had to drive Josh everywhere - since his Dad had died and she was alone. But, somehow she didn't mind. Today, they'd have to hurry to get home, get dressed and make it to graduation. Wouldn't his father be proud she thought.

At 2:30, Mary Spenser parked her car at the end of the

parking lot and started towards the front door when she saw Josh sitting on the front fender of Jake's car. He looked pale and shaken.

Jake spoke up, "We took care of it. Mrs. Spenser. They didn't do nothin to him." A glow of satisfaction emanated from his stocky frame.

"Who?" she said defensively as if she had visited this place before.

"The guys from Hebron, the track team guys — they started yelling names at Josh. You know, 'retard stuff'. And they started to push him around, you know." Jake shifted his weight from one foot to the other as he explained.

"We nailed em," said Harry from inside the car as he nursed a swollen fist. He stayed in the back seat in case the principal came out and noticed his fist. No fighting on school grounds.

Jake awkwardly gave Josh's arm a false punch and said, "We told em, Josh was our friend and they better leave him alone. Harry nailed the guy who pushed him and he ran away. They won't bother Josh again!"

Mrs. Spenser knew she should report the incident to the front office but didn't want Harry to get in trouble. She asked Jake what he thought and he simply said, "Naw, we'll take care of Josh. No one will touch him from now on."

Somehow this mother knew that having friends like Jake and Harry was more important than police reports and reports to the principal. It ended there!

Josh had been accepted for college and his mother knew that things might be better there. She took him to the barbershop for his haircut and they stopped at McDonald's for a burger before graduation. By the time Josh finished his Big Mac and fries, he was laughing at the way Harry hit the guy.

No one could escape the influence of Josh's infectious laughter. Especially his mother. He would suck in huge gulps of air, say something funny, and explode in another fit of laughter. Soon all of MacDonald's was smiling in their direction.

BACK ON KICK HILL ROAD

The EMT's got the accident victim on a gurney, cut through the white silk dress and closed the chest wound so that no air would get into the lungs. "Might have punctured the lung." one said.

Linda started the oxygen. The oxygen mask moved ever so slightly. Larry found a warm blanket to cover his teacher. "She's losing ground, the pulse is up and the pressure is thready." one attendant said when she read her pressure. "We need Life Star."

As Jenny Anderson was lifted onto the gurney, she felt an uneasy time shift. It was almost as if she had a deadline - for the yearbook, for the AP Test, for the vocabulary quiz — and she couldn't meet that deadline. There were too many kids lined up in front of her.

Then she remembered Josh's mother and the fire in her eyes when she defended Josh, and the tenderness in Josh's voice when he spoke of his "Mom". She saw Eric and his parents and it was as if someone had put a warm blanket over her. All the parents were helping her stack yearbooks, correcting quizzes and handing out paper for the test. What we need, Jenny thought, is more POSITIVE

PARENTAL INVOLVEMENT. The VOICE of EDUCATION chimed in:

"QUALITY KIDS COME FROM QUALITY PARENTS!" WE NEED BETTER **QUALITY CONTROL OF THE PRODUCTS** IN OUR SCHOOL

BUT THERE IS NO WAY TO CONTROL WHAT PARENTS DO TO HELP OR DAMAGE THEIR KIDS.

IF YOU SUGGEST A PROBLEM OR TRY TO HELP THE PRODUCT, SOME PARENTS WILL GO TO **COURT** AND BRING A **CIVIL LAWSUIT** AGAINST THE SCHOOL OR TEACHER. MOST OF THE TIME ALL YOU CAN DO IS IGNORE THE DAMAGE, AND PRETEND IT'S NOT THERE.

SOMETIMES **PARENTS** DAMAGE THEIR PRODUCTS AT HOME AND SEND THEM TO THE FACTORY HOPING WE CAN FIX THEM. PARENTS ABUSE OR NEGLECT THEIR PRODUCTS AND DENY THEY DO IT. THEY SEND SOME SO BROKEN WE CAN'T POSSIBLE GIVE THEM AN **EDUCATION**.

LIKE THE **FATHER** WHO CONTROLS, BELITTLES AND BERATES HIS SENSITIVE, WELL MANNERED SON SO THAT HE CAN'T THINK OR LEARN WITHOUT CONFUSION. COULD IT BE THAT THIS BRUTAL MAN IS RIDDLED WITH HOMOPHOBIA OR PERHAPS A LATENT HOMOSEXUALITY? COULD HE BE THE ONE WHO FEARS HOMOSEXUALITY IN HIMSELF AND, THEREFORE, IN HIS SON? HOW CAN THE SCHOOL SYSTEM CONTROL THIS SITUATION?

LIKE THE **MOTHER** WHO CONTROLS HER DAUGHTER WITH HER MISTRUST. SHE FEARS SHE

WILL BECOME PROMISCUIOUS AND END UP LIKE HER WHEN SHE WAS YOUNG. WILL THAT HAPPEN? PROBABLY HER FIRST INKLING WILL BE THE SEXULLY TRANSMITTED DISEASE THAT THEIR FAMILY DOCTOR WILL TREAT WHEN HER DAUGHTER ADMITS THAT SHE'S BEEN INVOLVED IN SEX. HOW CAN THE SCHOOL SYSTEM CONTROL THIS SITUATION?

WHO WILL BE THE ONE TO WARN THE PARENTS WHEN THEY SEE POTENTIAL PROBLEMS? WHO WILL BE THE ONES TO LET THE PARENTS KNOW THAT **THEY** MIGHT BE THE PROBLEM. THERE IS NO WAY FOR A SCHOOL SYSTEM TO DEMAND POSITIVE PARENTAL INVOLVEMENT OR MAKE UP FOR BAD PARENTING.

THE PAST JOURNEY

OCTOBER 10TH – PARENTS' NIGHT

Pulling into the parking lot, she checked to see if her designated space was open. Of course, not. No numbered spaces tonight. Over here by the ball field will have to do. Parent-teacher night again.

Clutching her green "grade" book to her chest, Mrs. Anderson edged her way out of the car just barely remembering to flip the lights switch before she slammed the door shut. A dead battery wouldn't do tonight.

Once inside the foyer, she hurried up to her room. Just in time! She put her name on the board and leaned on the desk.

Her green "grade" book was still clutched to her chest. It was her talking point tonight. She just needed to remember the class period of all 130 students. Oh, yes, Hilda Smith, Period Two. Hilda wasn't hard. Only had one Hilda.

Most conferences were terrific. What more can you say about a perfect all A student, who plays by all the rules, and is a joy to have in class? Those parents came in droves.

The tough ones were the ones when you had to say, "Mary needs to get her homework in or she probably won't make it this semester."

The usual defensive response, "She tells us she doesn't have any homework."

There isn't much to say to that except to repeat that, "Mary needs to get her homework in or she probably won't make it this semester." Usually, those parents don't come in droves.

Once in awhile Jenny Anderson would run into a set of parents that didn't seem to be talking about their own kid. This night was no exception.

Chet Bartlett, a huge man whose presence dominated the room, walked in first. Serious and full of business, he came close to where she was standing causing her to step back. His wife, hung back and Mrs. Anderson could see Jim, their son, hovering about in the corridor outside her room.

Jim was one of those boys who kind of evaporated into the back of the room - yet he was "with you" all the way. A good build, dark curly hair, chiseled good looks, a naturally gentle kid. How could you not enjoy teaching this kid?

His burly father forged ahead. "How's Jim doin?"

"Very well, Mr. Bartlett. Let's see, Period 2." she said

confidently turning to the names on the Period 2 page. "Right now his average is 87." A quick look across the row of numbers - no spaces. "His work is up to date."

She smiled when she thought of the way he was in class and gestured towards the boy confined to the corridor. "Jim's a pleasure to have in class."

It was as if the father never heard her!

"Well, if he gives you any trouble, you call me!" His voice reminded me of a disgruntled wrestler, one you would never tangle with, in or out of the ring. She stepped back again.

"But, Mr. Bartlett, Jim's doing very well in my class."

"We've always supported Jim's teachers and we'll take care of any problems you might have."

"But, Mr. Bartlett, he's a fine boy."

"Ok, but if he gives you any trouble, you call me."

The mother cringed wordlessly behind the father and Jim paced vacantly in the hall. Somewhat satisfied the father saw other parents waiting and made his way out into the hall to join his son.

Mrs. Anderson thought why couldn't she make that father see his son as she did - a wonderful boy with character and a refined sense of self-discipline? She thought his father needed to see him in school and observe him in a class where there were some "real" trouble-makers. How could she tell him that his son didn't have it in his nature to be a trouble-maker? What was the problem here?

The only thing she could think of was that this father couldn't possibly understand Jim's basic personality and was judging him by some other standard? An older child? His boyhood experiences? His own temperament? He simply did not understand his son. Innately, no matter what she said she knew he might never understand. She wondered if there wasn't more to Jim's story.

Her next set of parents, the Bermans, were involved parents who seemed to understand their kids. Mrs. Berman, who was the president of the Parent's Coalition, a group of parent advisors who met weekly with the principal, was incredibly active in school procedures. Mr. Berman, a member of the local school board, was an equally active participant in local education.

Eric Berman was in Mrs. Anderson's Advanced Placement class that met period four. Eric's parents were responsible and obviously they had helped their son to be the same. As parents, they kept a low profile and let Eric make his own decisions.

That night when they came into her parent conference, they remained quiet offering no suggestions. It was clear they always expected their son to handle his own life responsibly. He did!

ERIC - THE THIRD PRODUCT

To say that Eric was an exceptional student would be an understatement! He came to Mrs. A.'s Advanced Placement class and sat in the last seat in the back row. However, that was not where he placed in the class.

His written essays were exceptional, he answered difficult questions in class, and always had his work done on time. When Jenny Anderson saw how exceptional his writing was, she knew she needed him to be the Yearbook Editor-In-Chief.

Mrs. Ross, a young energetic art teacher, who started

the yearbook with her in the fall decided to move to Rhode Island when her husband was transferred there. She was the expert: Mrs. Anderson, the apprentice. Eric came to her rescue.

The yearbook kids always gathered in the art room in the old building. There were half thrown pots on the wheel; sculptures of odd looking subjects staring off in space and beautiful floral watercolors about the room. The Yearbook Kids spread a blank piece of paper on the paint stained table and struggled with the high backless stools.

"What about the lay-out for this section?" Mrs. A. anxiously asked pointing to the empty pages. Becky and Helene stared blankly in space.

"Becky's doing the Senior Section," Eric interjected. "Any decision, Becky?" Becky respected Eric and didn't want to disappoint him. Reluctant to share her half done project, she sneaked it out of her back pack.

"Don't know if you'll like this"– she qualified as she began to explain all the boxes and lines on her paper. "I think we should give each senior a half page with a candid and their description of themselves. We may have to take three or four pages from someplace else to do it but I think it's worth it."

Eric leaned in to check the project. "Great, Becky. You've really fixed it up. With the candid in here we've eliminated the old 'straight senior picture look', you know, the ones like every yearbook. We'll make the space somehow."

"But what if kids don't do the comments? You know, kids like Abe Pierson who never do nothin?" Jessica asked.

"If we get any kids who don't send in comments, we'll just insert some candid pictures." Eric held up the page and looked at it from a distance. "This really looks great." Eric leaned back in the chair and looked approvingly at Becky. She had to admit his blond hair and blue eyes really impressed her but she knew he had Leslie, the dark pretty one who always met him at lunch.

Becky smiled, pushed her shoulders back and sat up straight on the stool. The late bus bell rang and Helene moved uneasily in her seat. "Give me a ride," she mouthed to Jessica on the other side of the room. "OK" came back to her. Eric didn't worry about the bell because he knew his mother would pick him up later when he called her.

"Any decisions, Helene?"

"Yeah, right here." Slowly she unveiled her layout pages all done meticulously with art work for each sport and activity. Eric's usually serious face lit up.

"Helene, baby, you rock." Eric said approvingly. Helene blushed as she stepped back to let Eric and Mrs. A. turn the pages in front of them. A smudge of paint bled over onto the corner of one page. Lovingly, Helene wiped the edge.

"I'm impressed, you guys are great." the teacher added. They worked until the sun set and the room filled with an early dusky darkness. They were squinting to see the pages when Jessica finally turned on the lights and looked at her watch. "Hey, 5:30 I gotta go," she said motioning to Helene.

Eric had proven once again that he could get things done. He followed through as the Editor-In-Chief of the yearbook and as a member of the Advanced Placement class. He proved to be dependable and motivated. During the year, Mrs. Anderson encouraged Eric to submit some of his writing to a publisher and he got his name in print.

In a piece entitled "Peer Pressure; When the Choices are Difficult" he wrote: "High school is filled with distractions.

From sports to drama club, there are endless activities to be involved in and being involved in these activities is vital to your success. A large percentage of students who become heavily involved in drugs, alcohol, sex, do so out of boredom. This group of kids simply goes to school and comes home from school, and does nothing else. This excess "lag time" is a gate way for abuse."

It was obvious that Eric had used his time extremely well when the school announced that he would be the Valedictorian for this graduating class.

IN THE PRESENT

JUNE 10ᵀᴴ - GRADUATION DAY MORNING 10 AM - ERIC MEETS MRS ANDERSON TO PRACTICE HIS SPEECH

The rows of folding chairs and the stage were visible as Eric pulled into the Town hall parking lot. He was driving his father's green Toyota truck today because his mother wanted to get his car cleaned for tonight's graduation party. The speech he had written was in a folder on the front seat beside him. The loose pages tumbled out on the front seat beside him as he jerked to a stop.

"Mrs. A.'s not here yet," he said aloud as he reached for the tan folder. He flipped through the pages reading quickly repeating only the sections he had underlined for emphasis.

"As high school students, we're surrounded every day by many people who care about us – our teachers, mentors, and family members who have been there to look out for us. And most importantly we have had our parents who have been there for us. Let us take this opportunity to thank these important people for bringing us to this day, our graduation day."

A deep breath – "for bringing us to this day." Pause – "our graduation day."

Eric looked at his watch, "10 O'CLOCK – Hope I got the time right."

Just at that moment Mrs. Anderson pulled in beside him and waved her hand in a half circle. She turned off the motor and pulled the key from the ignition, thinking how proud she was of him – the yearbook, his writing and now Valediction. She didn't have senior classes today so she scheduled this meeting with Eric; then, she would finish up at the school and go home to get dressed for graduation.

She opened her car door and leaned over the top of her car. "Ready?"

Eric smiled as he gathered up his speech and joined her. They walked quickly around the brick building to the front of the village green and the stage where the microphone was set up. She ran to keep up with his long strides.

"Mr. Sergent promised me this mike would be up and running by Ten o'clock. Let's see. Testing, testing, 1-2-3." She said as she flicked her fingernail on the head of the microphone. The sound amplified and reached out to the empty seats.

"Great", she said. The teacher in her needed to give a few last minute instructions to a boy who had used a microphone on many occasions. She knew that but she also knew from other graduations that all Valedictorians can get nervous.

"Just relax and take a minute to set the mike, Eric." She

showed him the round silver disk and unscrewed it, moved it, only to screw it in place again. He watched her.

Eric's father was of German descent and his legacy to his son was a strongly featured face with a wide nose and full lips. His blue eyes softened his Slavic good looks and his blond hair made him seem younger that he was.

Eric stepped up to the mike and adjusted it to his six-foot frame as he visualized how he would speak that night.

"Just start to speak – any place. I'll go back and listen for volume."

Mrs. Anderson backed up through the middle aisle, the same aisle where the seniors would march in procession. For a moment, she envisioned the steely blue gowns for the boys and the sharp white ones for the girls. She could almost hear the familiar steady rhythm of "Pomp and Circumstance". A wave of sadness washed over her but she pushed back the emotion returning to Eric's speech, "bringing us to this day –our Graduation Day." Suddenly, she realized he had to hike the volume up.

Quickly, she moved down the aisle to where he stood. "How's that?" he asked.

"Ok, but we don't want to lose the back row. This sound system is the best we can do outdoors, so you'll have to adapt. Move in closer on the mike." She stepped up closer to Eric and said, "I always tell the kids to 'kiss the mike. Not literally but figuratively'." He smiled thinking of the metaphors, similes and figures of speech she had pasted around her room.

"OK, try it again."

Again, she scurried off to the back row.

"Every person holds their destiny in their own hands

and can accomplish and achieve all they desire. But you can only do this with the right focus, the right tools, and the right attitude. I like to refer to attitude as the 'compass' of the human spirit." Now his voice was strong and clear.

Mrs. Anderson listened, then, nodded her head in his direction. He recognized the look of approval on her face and went on to define the "right focus", the "right tools" and, most eloquently, the "right attitude." Sitting alone in one of the empty chairs in the back row, she became his only audience as the mid-day sun heated up the morning.

When he finished, the village green heard the clapping of one pair of hands. Unlike the applause to be heard there that evening, this sound said, "Great job, Eric! You're exceptional! You've done it again! You've been a pleasure to know and to teach! And good-bye to this part of your life. And good-bye to a wonderful part of mine."

"Thanks Mrs. A.," he said as he moved toward his father's green truck. "See you tonite at 6:30." And he was gone.

LESLIE - THE FOURTH PRODUCT

Eric thought of his girlfriend Leslie. She was the dark pretty girl who sat in the third row of Mrs. Anderson's AP Class. Every day she met Eric at lunch and they talked to their friends. It was a mixed group – some kids from Leslie's art class and a couple of guys from the baseball team.

Leslie and Eric had been "going out" since sophomore year and this year they were crowned King and Queen of the Prom. Everyone knew them as a "cute couple". No one bothered them and they pretty much stuck together.

Leslie lived in a condo with her mother on the west side of Heritage. Her parents were divorced so she was extremely close to her mother. They talked about everything! When Sandy Schroeder saw that Leslie and Eric were falling

in love, she helped her get birth control pills because she didn't want her daughter to face an unwanted pregnancy.

Leslie loved art. At eight years old, her mother took her for private lessons every Saturday. Then, it grew into lessons at the YMCA, and a summer art camp at the university. Finally, during high school, she was taking college courses in portrait and watercolor at the University of Vermont. Art was Leslie's passion, besides Eric, of course. She had been accepted with a full scholarship at Rhode Island School of Design and would be going there in the fall. Eric would be at Brown University so they could get together on weekends.

After practicing his speech, Eric went to work – to earn all he could for college. Tonight, Eric would pick up Leslie and they would go to his house to get ready for graduation. Eric's mother had things all ready when they arrived.

She had ordered pizza so they had something to eat before "the big night". They both grabbed a slice as they hurried to get ready. Soon, after a quick hug and kiss for "MOM", they were out the door.

"My Mom got my car washed today," Eric said absently as he opened the door for Leslie to get in. She hurried knowing he couldn't be late. His newly ironed blue gown was carelessly draped over his arm with his cap set to one side on his head. Quickly, without a word, she took the cap and gown from him and laid them carefully on the back seat. She hung her white gown on the side hook behind his seat. A florist box with a single red rose was on the floor.

"For you," he said nodding toward the rose.

"You're so sweet," she kissed him quickly on the cheek

as they roared out of the driveway.

"No, you are," he answered smiling at her, loving the look of her long dark hair, her green eyes and that friendly face. Suddenly, he knew how much he would miss her. She had the same thought and tightly held his hand as they drove past Heritage High – to graduation, to get their diplomas so that they could go to different colleges. So, that they could leave each other. The thought was unbearable.

BACK ON KICK HILL ROAD

Larry knew they didn't have much time! What made Larry Blaisdell brilliant was his productivity. He had the ability "to figure things out, to get things done" when everyone else was disoriented and confused. After all, he was a farmer. When you care for animals, you've got to "think smart." Larry had birthed many a hog, cured their sickness, and brought them to slaughter. He knew how to get things done!

"That copter ain't gonna get in here – not on this stretch of road," he said to Jed almost as if Jed wasn't there.

"We got to go up past Emmett's garage to the clearing near Hayward's barn. Only level land around. I'll get us there!" He shouted.

After Linda gave Larry the thumbs up, he carefully, skillfully picked his way up the paved road, jumped out of the ambulance to remove a wooden fence post and continued on the worn grassy road to the open field. The sharp siren sound startled onlookers, moving them out of his way.

In the distance, they could see Life star hovering overhead; hesitating, moving away, then, turning back to the clearing. Without the interference of electrical lines, telephone wires, onlookers, auxiliary police, and fire trucks; the plane made a timely, perfect landing.

Despite the screaming sirens and the drone of the helicopter THE VOICE OF EDUCATION still clamored to be heard:

WE NEED TO BALANCE THE BUDGET! - THE TOWN TAKES IN 150 TUITION STUDENTS @ 7,000 DOLLARS FOR EACH STUDENT FROM **THE STATE OF VERMONT**. THAT ADDS ONE MILLION AND FIFTY THOUSAND DOLLARS TO **THE SCHOOL BUDGET**. BUT THE TEACHERS CAN'T POSSIBLE RUN THAT MANY PRODUCTS THROUGH THE ASSEMBLY LINE AND CREATE EDUCATED PRODUCTS. MOST OF **THE TOWN** DOESN'T CARE BECAUSE THEY HAVE FOUND A WAY TO KEEP THEIR **TAXES** FROM GOING UP.

SOME **"DEDICATED" TEACHERS** STILL BELIEVE THEY CAN FIND <u>5 MINUTES</u> EACH WEEK TO CORRECT EACH PRODUCT'S PAPERS. FOR 130 STUDENTS, THAT IS, AN EXTRA TEN HOURS OF **CORRECTING** AT HOME EACH WEEK. TWO HOURS, MONDAY – TWO HOURS, TUESDAY- TWO HOURS, WEDNESDAY – TWO HOURS, THURSDAY – TWO HOURS, ON THE WEEK-END.

TEACHERS ARE WEARING OUT FROM **THE WORK LOAD**, WITH A DISEASE CALLED **BURN-OUT.** SOME USE **SICK DAYS** JUST TO SURVIVE. SOME LEAVE OR RETIRE IF THEY CAN. CLASSES

ARE BECOMING UNMANAGEABLE; KIDS ARE FALLING OFF THE ASSEMBLY LINE AS **DROP OUTS**. THE **TEACHER'S UNION** THREATENS TO **STRIKE** AND STOP THE ASSEMBLY LINE ALTOGETHER.

THE PUBLIC IS ENRAGED THAT THEIR TEACHERS WOULD COMPLAIN. THE PRODUCTS KEEP GETTING PUSHED INTO A SMALLER SPACE ON THE CONVEYOR BELT. LESS BOOKS, MORE DESKS IN THE ROOM. MANY JUST SLIP OFF AND NEVER GET EDUCATED.

LEAVING KICK HILL ROAD

IN THE LIFE STAR HELICOPTER

In the Life Star Helicopter, the nurse talked to Jenny to try to pull her back to consciousness. Jenny began to shiver. A white and red silk dress lay in scraps on the floor.

"Check her pupils – any reaction?" "Start the glucose and water – saline" "Can't get in – will have to cut down."

"We have an accident victim with severe trauma – in and out of consciousness. May have internal bleeding, shallow breathing. Pressures's holding. We'll hurry." The door shut out the onlookers on the ground. Linda and Larry watched helplessly from below.

Jenny Anderson slipped into a deeper darkness as the numbers on the pressure gauge slipped lower. Her heart beat was slower now.

"She's slipping away!"

Latisha, she slipped away. Mrs. A. remembered her student, Latisha. She tried to tell them, "We couldn't help her. She needed to go to college." Past time blended with the present moment as Mrs. A. drifted back to when Latisha came to her AP class.

THE PAST JOURNEY

NOVEMBER 10th – THE FOURTH CLASS OF THE DAY - ADVANCED PLACEMENT - ENGLISH

In November, Latisha Emmons showed up in the Period 4 – AP Class. She was one of three African American kids in the senior class. Having gone to Norwich Academy for three years, she decided to move to Heritage to live with Damon, her boyfriend, and finish her last year here. In moving she gave up her 4.0 average and her first place in the graduating class there. Therefore, she was placed in AP courses.

Latisha took the AP class by storm. Her dark beauty was captivating, her quick mind electrifying, and her ability to read the literature aloud with clarity and emphasis was astounding. In all her years of teaching, Mrs. Anderson had never seen such presence and command. Clearly, Latisha was the most capable student in the room.

When Mrs. A. introduced to the class Toni Morrison's, Beloved, a story of sorrow and slavery, Latisha was in her element. She was asked to read and interpret the text - not because of her African American roots, but because she could handle the difficulty of the text.

Ultimately, Mrs. Anderson asked Latisha to record her readings so she could use them in other classes. Latisha had a natural presence and command of language that was exceptional. Soon, she was asked to record Beowulf, Chaucer, and King Lear – all to be used in the other classrooms. She got extra credit for her work. It was clear Latisha could have an amazing career in media communications.

As it turned out, Latisha could easily have retained her 4.0 average and taken Eric's place as Valedictorian but around January she began to miss school on Fridays. Then it was Fridays and Mondays. She always had a note, written by her emancipated self, saying she had been sick but soon the attendance committee got impatient with her. She lost some credit in AP Chemistry and French 111.

LATISHA – THE FIFTH PRODUCT

When she turned eighteen in September, she became legal and could pretty much live where she wanted to. Damon, who was twenty six and needed some help with the expenses, convinced her that she could work four nights a week at Heritage's busiest restaurant, The Chowder House. Her tips were good and she could finish up school and make good money at the same time. It would all work out!

Since Latisha hated living with her step father and mother, she grabbed the chance. She loved Damon, who worked on and off on construction jobs, and loved their little apartment over by the reservoir in Heritage.

As the year progressed, Mrs. Anderson could see that Latisha was in a terrible struggle with her life in school and her life outside of school. One overcrowded the other. She missed a few key assignments and her overall average fell.

When it came time to take Heritage High School's Comprehensive Exit Exam for graduation, it was no surprise to Mrs. A. that Latisha got the highest score in the class. She did not receive any credit for that on her average but it assured her graduation from high school.

In May, when it came time to take the AP English Literature test, she and Eric got a 5, a perfect score. Eric would get college credit for that score from Brown University where he had been accepted in early decision; Latisha had not applied to college. She said, "I'm going to take a year off". That's what she told Mr. Gray, the overworked Guidance Counselor, and Mr. McManus, the concerned Principal. When they offered to contact a college in her behalf, she insisted that she was firm in her decision.

No one ever knew why she had made that decision: her relationship with Damon, or plans to be married, or perhaps the desire to have children, very limited or no finances for college – none of, or some of the above. Perhaps she simply refused to start a new life that might leave Damon behind.

People respected and admired Latisha, but were intimidated by her apparent maturity and the power of her presence, so they refused to ask questions. She graduated fifth in the class but was not eligible to give a speech at the graduation.

On graduation night, Damon, uncomfortable and out of his element in this predominately "white" academic gathering, watched her get her diploma from his seat in the back row. They left together immediately after the ceremony. They didn't notice the life star helicopter flying overhead.

LEAVING KICK HILL ROAD

IN THE LIFE STAR HELICOPTER

With a thumbs up from Larry, the copter pilot lifted the bulky bird skyward.

The motion of the helicopter shook Jenny. She was uncomfortable. First, she felt like it was a crisp, cold autumn afternoon. Then, the warmth of being covered by the summer sun. It was as if she had been stripped naked. An <u>uneasiness</u> crept over her as her whole body started to shake.

The nurse pulled back her eyelids to see if her pupils were big and fixed. "She's slipping away!" an alarmed voice said. Someone said the word "hypovolemia" and the teacher began to spell it in her mind — hypo–vol-e-mia. She knew with that word someone must be very sick!

She tried to yell out "Frank is sick! He needs help!" In the darkness no one heard her! Time shifted back to the fall of the year.

THE PAST JOURNEY

DECEMBER 10ᵗʰ — THE FIFTH CLASS OF THE DAY - LEVEL TWO- ENGLISH

6:30 Am — the leaves, red, mustard and wine, had fallen to the ground — just waiting for the first snow. Each farm in Heritage had taken on its own Winslow Homer quality. As

Mrs. Anderson drove to the School Factory, she noticed the Abbott farm on the left. The white house had long ago lost its clean look. The paint was peeling on the barn.

"They say Frank Sargent lives in a shack behind the barn," she said vacantly to the only living thing in sight, two black and white cows grazing in the muddy field. She wondered if his house was visible from the road. She arched her head to the left. Guess not. Then she thought of her period five class and wondered if Frank would be there.

The level two class came charging in after lunch — thirty four strong with loud voices. The guys hit each other on the back affectionately as they remembered the all-star football game over the week-end. The girls talking to each other about the party after the game. Attendance — 4 kids missing!

So, let's begin. After about 15 minutes of a laborious discussion of Chaucer's Canterbury Tales, the class broke into groups and Mrs. Anderson moved from group to group like a waitress in a busy diner.

"What do we do with # C.? I don't get it."

"OK, that's the part that goes back to p. 62 in your book. Here-"she said as she flipped the pages to 62. "Right here – you outline this section and pick it up at page 98." Again she flipped the pages.

"OK, Ok I got it!"

Out of the corner of her eye she could see Frank eyeing Stacey who was in his group. His hand was up.

"What does it mean when it says 'time chart'?" Frank said directing the question to the teacher in his loudest voice but still looking at Stacey.

"OK, you go back to the Introduction and take the

most important dates and events and line them up in a chart." Mrs. Anderson rummages through the file folder she carried and put a paper down on Frank's desk.

"Like this." "OK, I got it."

Frank settled down in his seat for a minute looking at the time chart. Then, he pushed his seat very close to Stacey. His tanned face stood out in obvious contrast to his short curly bleached blond hair. His clothes smelled of the black and white cows from the Abbott farm. Frank reached over Stacey's chest, just missing her, to get the ruler on her desk. She pulled way back.

"Thank you, Kitty." Frank said seductively.

Stacey, a buxom cheerleader, winced when she heard the word "Kitty." Everyone knew what Frank meant when he called girls "kitty." The word really started with P but he would be expelled if he used that word in school so he used the other.

Matt was talking to a girl in his group at the back of the room pretending to be completing a project while she really did all the work. His head lifted when he heard Frank say "Kitty" and he laughed knowingly; the girl beside him laughed a little too just to go along. She was just hoping that Frank wouldn't "Kitty" her next.

Mrs. Anderson was offended and enraged at the same time. She had let it go for weeks now and knew she had to act. I'm going to talk to him after class she decided and if that doesn't work he's going to the Principal.

Edging over to Frank's side of the room just one minute before the bell, Mrs. A. caught Frank and redirected him back into the classroom. She knew she didn't have much time between classes so she was blunt and direct.

"The girls are afraid of you, Frank. Do you know

that?"

"What do you mean?" he moved defensively.

"Well, they won't say anything because they're afraid. They know what you mean when you say 'Kitty'." Mrs. A moved behind the desk and Frank sat perched on the edge of the first chair in the row. A wry smile crept up over his face as he adopted the look of an innocent farm boy who was just teasing, having fun.

"I'm just having fun with them," he said as he verbalized his body language. Anyone else might have believed him and let him go but not Mrs. Anderson who was known to be a teacher you couldn't fool.

"They're afraid of you, Frank." She persisted. "Everyone has a right to their own sexual identity and you have no right to use sexual terms that make the girls uneasy."
"Well. I….."

"Frank," she said in a softer voice, "I see a lot from up here behind this desk. You thought I wouldn't say anything because it's about sex - but I don't want to see you hurt these girls."
"But they like it!"

"Frank, they don't like it. They're afraid. You're asking me and the rest of the class to accept your sexual references. The guys laugh but they wouldn't like you to say that to their girlfriends."
"I didn't think it hurt anyone."

"I know you didn't. There are some really shy girls in this class and I think they have a right to learn about sexual things at their own pace."

Frank shifted uneasily and blushed for the first time. He looked toward the door to see if any kids might be coming in.

"I know it's better to learn by yourself. I was sexually molested by my step mother when I was about 12. I don't know but maybe that's why I keep saying these things."

There was a silence and in that silence the bell rang. The moment was gone! Stunned, Mrs. Anderson knew she had to arrange a meeting with the principal to talk about Frank.

FRANK - THE SIXTH PRODUCT

When Frank's father and stepmother threw him out of the house, Mr. Abbott offered him a place to stay until he graduated. He would let Frank stay in the little out-building behind the barn if he would do some farm work. He knew that Frank was tough - a good worker.

Before school, Frank milked the cows and tended the animals. A barnyard odor followed him through his day at the School Factory. No one liked to stand too close to Frank. He had a muscular build and bright blond hair that screamed "Notice me." The hair might have been from sitting in the sun on the tractor but more than likely Frank had some friend bleach it.

Frank knew no boundaries with his hair or anything else. There was a merry jauntiness about him, a kind of "I don't care about anyone in the world and you'd better watch out for me" attitude. Most of the kids felt sorry for Frank because they knew he scrounged around for food. He'd show up for every free meal in town. Sometimes at lunch the kids gave him their food.

Frank's situation with his step mother had left him marked for life. These sexual encounters may have been the only attention he got that felt like love. He never knew his mother because she died when he was four, and his father never knew how to show him love. In the end, sex was what he came to think of as love - and sex was his obsession!

One night some guys from school became curious about what Frank did at night living alone in that shack. They probably thought he had a girl with him or something. They stole out to the Abbott's farm and carefully picked their way to the back of the fields. A window was lit; they could see Frank inside. The rumor was he was alone masturbating. They saw Playboy magazines strewn all over the filthy floor.

The guys laughed at Frank especially when he called the girls "Kitty." Sometimes he'd say "Pretty Kitty", "Pamela Kitty," "Jenny Kitty" but he could always get the guys to laugh and it relieved the boredom, distracted the class, bothered the teacher, and generally kept things going.

Usually, if a guy didn't laugh at Frank they might not be considered a "real" guy. Homophobic boys usually laughed loudest.

Then Frank was missing from school for about three weeks. It was no surprise to Mrs. Anderson when Frank came back to class bragging of having been in Florida with a 45 year old married woman. The guys thought it was funny and the girls were disgusted.

After class, Mrs. A. stopped Frank to talk to him about the work he had missed. She hit the subject immediately.

"What's the deal? You were in Florida with this married lady?" she opened the dialogue.

"Where's her husband?"

"He was there too. Yeah, she's good to me," he said sheepishly.

"I'm no fool, Frank, what's the deal? You're with some woman – married, 45 years old? And her husband goes along?" she persisted.

"Well, she likes me, you know." he smiled that wry smile.

"You mean sexually."

"Yeah, I turned 18 you know. Stayed back in the second grade. So, I'm legal." He divulged almost before he himself knew it.

"But she's too old for you – think about it Frank," she countered not immediately realizing the full impact of Frank's admissions. The bell rang and Frank stopped talking. The teacher turned to the book in her hand and quickly sketched out what homework he would have to do to pass this semester.

That was the last conversation about sex that Jenny Anderson had with Frank. For the most part, he stopped calling the girls "kitty" in her class. But she noticed there was only one girl that Frank had never called "Kitty" and that was Sylvia.

When Mrs. A. asked Sylvia about Frank, Sylvia told her that she lived next door to Abbott's farm and some afternoons she would ride around the fields on the tractor with Frank.

SYLVIA - THE SEVENTH PRODUCT

Sylvia Smith was in Frank's Level Two Class Period Five. Somehow, he noticed her but never bothered her; she seemed to laugh off his remarks to others. They were neighbors and she wasn't afraid of him.

One day Sylvia told Mrs. A. she wanted to go to modeling school. Basically, her ambition wasn't too far out of range. She already carried herself like she was on a runway.

Her head held high, an engaging smile, she maneuvered her 5'7" frame in and out of the room. A natural model!

The only problem was that Sylvia had a secret hole inside that couldn't be filled. Her life stopped at eight when her father incested her. Since that time she was subject to panic attacks and suffered intense anxiety. Always on the edge of her nerves – if things didn't go her way she would revert to an inordinately intense anger. But she knew how to handle it. Several times she bolted from the room and went to the ladies room to cry. Mrs. Anderson always sent Alecia, her friend, to help her.

Sylvia lived with her mother over by the Abbott farm. She felt sorry for Frank so sometimes she went out to see him when he was alone plowing the field. They'd ride around on the tractor for awhile. He was just a friend. The other kids made fun of Frank behind his back saying he was "sex crazy" and talked dirty to the girls. She didn't believe it because Frank talked to her so nice.

Frank tried to warn her about "smoking weed" with Alicia, and hanging out with the "druggies" from Norwich Academy. She knew he was right but couldn't seem to get away from wanting to get high.

Then, one night in March it happened! Sylvia took her long flowing chestnut hair, her lovely smile, and her perfectly proportioned body to a rock concert in Norwich. The idea was to get wasted. And she did! Someone had some "ecstasy"! She tried it! Someone had some pills! She did those too! She got very high and forgot all about the pain inside.

On the way home, Matt, Alecia's boyfriend, was driving too fast, couldn't maneuver the curve, and smashed head-on into a tree. Alicia and Matt died instantly. Sylvia who was passed out in the back seat didn't feel it when the glass ripped into her pretty model's face. No magazine covers for Sylvia! She didn't realize it when the sharp metal took out her knees and ankle. No runways for Sylvia!

But that wasn't the most tragic part! The worst part was the head injury that was compounded by the mixture of drugs in her brain. Her coma wasn't a normal swollen brain kind that might eventually return her to a normal reality. Her coma occurred when her mind was altered by drugs and she woke up to find she had slipped out of "normal" completely. With little short term or long term memory left, she woke up long after they buried Matt and Alecia.

Frank reported her condition to the class every day. He told Mrs. A. how he sneaked in to talk to her every day even though she couldn't hear him. Even though the rule was "family only." Frank knew how to get things done without being noticed. Let's say he knew his way around.

He told the class the day Sylvia blinked her eyes and finally started to wake up. He told Mrs. A. that it was time for her to visit Sylvia. She went that night.

THE PAST JOURNEY

DECEMBER 24th - VISITING SYLVIA IN THE HOSPITAL

It was Christmas Eve. There was a Christmas tree and some decorations in the front foyer of the hospital. Everything on the ground floor seemed cheery, dressed in a merry red and green. Christmas music was softly playing.

But the smell of the hospital hit her as soon as she reached the fifth floor. The nurse on the desk directed her to Sylvia's room. Mrs. Anderson wasn't sure what she'd find in Rm. 521. Frank said Sylvia had come out of the coma and was awake but that was all.

Cautiously, she opened the heavy door pushing it slowly towards the girl in the bed. Sylvia's mother was pulling the pillow out from her head to make her more comfortable. She motioned the teacher in.

"Sylvia?" Mrs. A. said trying not to let on how unrecognizable she was. Nothing could have prepared her for the vacant look in Sylvia's eyes. Her beautiful face was heavily bandaged and her engaging smile turned crooked. Her mother looked away.

"How are you?"

"OK," she answered wearily.

"Don't talk. I just wanted to let you know that we all miss you and are thinking of you. The kids talk about you all the time."

A vacant look. A moment of recognition. Another vacant look. Then, she shut her eyes to sleep. The mother gestured Mrs. A. from the room.

"She's in and out." "I'm so sorry."

"I know. Everyone has been so good. Maybe in a few weeks she'll be more coherent." She shook her head and looked at the floor almost as if she hardly believed what she was saying. Almost as if she needed to express this vain hope just in case it could come true.

"I'll do what I can to help her get the credits to graduate. I've checked with guidance already. We'll talk soon."

Mrs. Anderson said knowing that she had the power to adjust the school work to Sylvia's level; also knowing that Sylvia was one of the seniors who came into the year with extra credits – one who needed only one English credit to graduate.

"Thank you so much."

When Jenny Anderson left the hospital, she felt much like she did after attending a funeral but this time the dead person was still alive.

Sylvia never came back to the regular classroom. Mrs. Anderson met with Sylvia each week. At first she read to her. Then, she was able to go over the test questions that the other kids were answering in class.

They went very, very slowly! Sylvia couldn't always understand or remember a whole book but she could handle a paragraph.

For a writing assignment, Sylvia dictated a journal all about the accident, the loss of her friend Alicia, the physical therapy, and the upcoming skin graph operations. Her fears, her feelings.

Finally, by June she could remember how to spell enough words to write a few simple sentences in her journal by herself. Frank was still visiting her every day. She was walking with a cane and smiling her new crooked smile. All talk of modeling school was gone. She was thankful to be alive – and to be able to graduate!

IN THE PRESENT

JUNE 10TH - GRADUATION DAY – EARLY

AFTERNOON - FRANK'S FATHER AND STEP MOTHER GETTING READY FOR GRADUATION.

It was early - just 4 pm he thought. Frank's father pulled the bottle of beer out of the refrigerator. When he did, he knocked a half-filled diet coke on the floor. The coke can twirled around on the linoleum as the brown fluid shot out hitting the baseboard and the legs of the stool.

"Jesus" he muttered. "Why did you leave that coke there? Half-full as usual." Madeline, who was perched on one of the stools, said nothing but moved her legs out of the way of the coke and kept on clipping her nails. Some of the nail clippings joined the coke on the floor.

"You having a beer?" she said changing the subject.
She handed him some paper towels.

"Yeah, you have any friggin problem with that?" He pushed the paper towel around the floor with his foot and looked directly at her.

"Tonight is graduation – Frank's graduation. Don't you think we should wait til after?"

He swigged his beer slowly telling himself it was OK to just have one.

"Never thought he'd make it. That fuckin kid has been nothing but trouble ever since Clara died. Good looking - but he just don't listen to nobody. Probably wants money – that's why he sent those tickets."

A brindled colored cat rubbed up against Madelaine's legs. She reached down and scooped the cat into her lap. Gently she stroked the hair on its neck.

"Yeah, he's good looking alright." The step mother noted. Then, she put the cat down, opened the refrigerator door and reached for a beer. The cap made a familiar comforting sound as it snapped back from the can.

"You talk about me! You're having a beer too." He laughed.

"Just one – can't stand to be sitting there with all the mucky-muck Heritage snobs. They make me sick. Maybe I shouldn't go, Carl."

Now Carl was settling into the recliner with his beer in one hand and the remote in the other. Carl was a tough 5"9" who weighed in about 185. Most of the time he was "drivin truck" – on the road. His hair was the color and consistency of molasses. Sometimes when he was on the road, he couldn't find a truck stop shower so he didn't get to wash his hair. Tonight, he'd have to wash it if he wanted to go to Frank's graduation.

Madelaine moved from her perch on the wooden stool to the arm of Carl's chair. She was a slim 130 pounds with curves in all the right places. Carl playfully touched her breast as she leaned into him. She pulled away.

"Do I have to go?" she teased. "You know I love Frank and all but I hate this town."

"No, ya don't have to do nothing ya don't want to do," he said defensively remembering the birthday party they had for her daughter last month. Her selfishness always came back to haunt him like a song you can't get out of your head. But he also knew that once Madelaine decided not to do something that was it. She leaned into him suggestively.

"Let's go to Rudy's and get a pizza and then we'll decide."

Carl had one more beer while he was taking a shower. Madelaine joined him in the shower. It was nearly 5:30 by the time they reached Rudy's. They had their usual pizza — pepperoni, mushroom and onions. When Rudy saw Carl and Madelaine, he insisted on buying them a beer. Just one for the road. An hour slipped by.

Around 6:30, the CB began squawking in the back room. Rudy went back to see what was happening. "A crash over on Kick Hill," he said excitedly to Carl and Madelaine. They ordered another beer as the sirens began to scream through town.

It was 7.30 when they left Rudy's so they decided not to go to the graduation but just drive by the Green to see if they could see Frank.

Carl and Madeline drove down Lindsey Road past the Old Cemetery and took a side road up to the Village Green. It brought them out by the side of the Green Store – a spot where they could see what was going on but not be seen. As they pulled up Tom Zabroski, Jr. was getting his diploma.
"There's Zabroski's–kid -we missed Frank," Carl said.

When Frank went up to get his diploma, some kids yelled out "Kitty, Kitty". None of the parents understood so they just smiled. All the graduates on the stage smiled. Mr. McManus, the Principal, looked down at his feet, straightened his back, and turned around to give the graduates a warning look. Their faces became serious again.

Right before the class turned their tassels on their caps, Frank thought he saw his father's truck pull out from the Green Store. He dismissed the thought. Probably in the back row he thought. He strained to see. No sight of them.

"What the hell?" he thought as he walked down the aisle behind his classmates. Nearly at the end, he tripped and fell into Sylvia who was walking unsteadily in front of him. Her hair brushed against his face and he touched her waist to steady her. She smiled over her shoulder – a crooked, silly smile!

BACK ON KICK HILL ROAD

The volunteer police told the onlookers to go on home. Speaking in whispered tones they huddled on the sidelines of the action. Somehow they thought they might help just by being there. One of them found a small white purse on the grass and gave it to a policeman.

"A teacher, on the way to graduation," one of them said. "Anderson I think they said. Senior high school teacher."

"Oh my God, I had her for English. Are you sure?"

"Yeah, she's been there awhile. Lives over on Thorndike Road."

"Drove that little Mazda. It blew up. She's got one kid in college. We graduated together in 2005. Robert Anderson – remember."

The conversation was interrupted when more ambulances came screaming in from Rutland and Norwalk. Larry and Linda told them they weren't needed - so they shut their sirens off and left.

The screaming sirens startled the mothers in the crowd making them disoriented like they used to when their own children cried in the middle of the night; making them realize they needed to get home to their kids.

Again, the VOICE OF EDUCATION tried to be heard shouting over the noisy scene.

"YOU SHOULD KNOW THAT PRODUCTS CAN REPRODUCE PRODUCTS! THERE ARE SOME **GIRLS** ON THE CONVEYOR BELT WHO GET IN **TROUBLE** BY GETTING TOO CLOSE TO THE **BOYS.** THEY REALLY END UP IN BIG TROUBLE!

SUZY HAS A TWO YEAR OLD BUT HER PARENTS SUPPORT HER. SHE IS IN THE **SUPER INTELLIGENT ASSEMBLY LINE** AND JUST WANTS TO MAKE IT TO **GRADUATION** SO SHE CAN GET A BETTER **JOB**. HER PARENTS HAVE BEEN TAKING CARE OF SUZY AND BABY BILLY SINCE SHE WAS SIXTEEN AND WILL CONTINUE TO UNTIL SUZY FINISHES COLLEGE AND BILLY IS SIX YEARS OLD.

SUZY'S **MOTHER** LOVES BILLY BUT IS TIRED OF STAYING HOME DURING THE DAY TO WATCH HIM. SHE'S TIRED OF CHANGING **DIAPERS** WHILE SUZY DOES HER HOMEWORK, PAYING FOR THE **BABY FOOD AND DIAPERS** AND GETTING UP TO FEED THE BABY AT NIGHT.

LORRY, SUZY'S VERY BEST FRIEND, WAS THERE WHEN SUZY BROUGHT BABY BILLY INTO SCHOOL FOR THE FIRST TIME. WHEN THE GIRLS BRING THE BABIES BACK TO THE SCHOOL FACTORY TO SHOW THEM OFF, ALL THE OTHER GIRLS LOOK WITH ENVY AT THE CUTE LITTLE BABIES. THEY SEE THEIR FRIENDS WITH A POSSESSION - **A BABY** WHO NEEDS THEM. IT'S ALL SO SEDUCTIVE - THE SEX ON THE ASSEMBLY LINE AND THE SWEET NEW BABY!

SO LORRY GOT PREGNANT, JUST LIKE HER FRIEND SUZY. SHE HAD A **BABY PRODUCT** IN

SEPTEMBER AND NEVER MADE IT BACK TO FINISH HER SENIOR YEAR. LORRY'S MOTHER KNEW SHE HAD **A SERIOUS BOYFRIEND** BUT WAS CONVINCED THAT LORRY'S RELIGIOUS BELIEF WOULD HELP HER TO ABSTAIN FROM SEX UNTIL MARRIAGE. FOR THAT REASON, OF COURSE, SHE NEVER MENTIONED **BIRTH CONTROL** TO LORRY.

LORRY WAS AN INTELLIGENT, CARING GIRL, SO SHE DECIDED TO STAY HOME AND BREAST FEED HER CHILD. HER DECISION WAS PROBABLY A GOOD ONE, BASED ON ALL THE LATEST BOOKS ON PREGNANCY AND CHILDBIRTH.

HOWEVER, NO ONE EVER TOLD LORRY THAT TO TAKE CARE OF A BABY, YOU HAVE TO HAVE **MONEY**. HER MOTHER, A WORKING SINGLE MOM, COULDN'T AFFORD TO PAY FOR THE CHILD. TO FILL IN, LORRY TOOK HER BREAST SWOLLEN BODY TO THE LATE NIGHT SHIFT AT WAL-MARTS.

MOST **YOUNG MOTHERS** DROP OFF THE BELT AND GO **HOME. SO,** OF COURSE, LORRY QUIT SCHOOL AND WON'T GRADUATE. AS A HIGH SCHOOL DROP OUT, SHE PROBABLY WON'T EVER GET A BETTER JOB THAN WAL-MARTS.

SUZY AND LORRY REMAINED BEST FRIENDS BUT DIDN'T HAVE MUCH TIME FOR EACH OTHER NOW THAT THEY BOTH HAD BABIES. THEN, IN JANUARY, SUZY AND JUSTIN'S LIFE FELL APART.

THE PAST JOURNEY

JANUARY 10ᵀᴴ - PERIOD TWO - LEVEL ONE ENGLISH

On the way to school, it started to snow. Not the soft kind but the kind with ice chips in it – the kind that lands on your windshield and slithers across the glass. The road was slippery. As she left the Donut Shop where she always stopped for an apple turnover, a snowplow pulled out in front of Jenny Anderson. She was able to piggyback behind the plow all the way to school.

When she passed Kick Hill Road, she remembered her Level 1 class last Friday. The kids were talking about the fight between Suzy's father and Justin Tobin.

"Yeah, Suzy's father was rip-shit! He carries a shot-gun in his truck too!" Phil whispered. Then, a quick look at the teacher because of the "shit" part. Mrs. A knew there was a time to pretend you hadn't heard the "shit" part and pay attention to the shot gun part.

"I heard the Tobin's think Suzy's to blame." Another kid offered as he leaned into the conversation. "Now, she won't let Justin see little Billy."

"Suzy's father went down to the quarry and found Justin and told him to stay away from Suzy and Billy."

"I thought we were all dead!" someone said looking at the door, almost half expecting Justin and Suzy to come into the class a little bit late like they always did. Not that Friday!

Suzy lived with her parents who had set up an apartment over the garage for her and little Billy. The Stevenson's didn't mind Justin stopping by to see his son and helping out but they wouldn't approve of a marriage.

When Justin wasn't visiting Suzy and Billy, he was

working six days a week over at Simond's Auto Body Shop on RT 11. On Sunday, Justin would take Suzy to the Laundromat in Willington where they would do the laundry. They always laughed a lot on Sunday's. Most of the time they just put little Billy right in the basket with the clean clothes. He laughed when they laughed.

After a while, the Stevenson's bought a new washing machine and dryer that they put in the garage so that Suzy could wash the baby's clothes. Suzy's mother didn't want Suzy to put Justin's greasy pants into the same washing machine as Billy's clothes so he did his own laundry on Sunday night. He didn't like to leave but he knew he needed to have clothes to work and needed to give money to Suzy. They would see each other the next day in class. For the most part, they seemed to be working things out.

Something must have happened – no one seemed to know!

When Mrs. Anderson got to school she went directly to Mr. McManus, the school principal, who was in his office standing over his desk looking intently through a folder of papers. A picture of his wife, Abbie, and their two girls, was strategically placed on the window ledge.

"Wanted to talk to you about Justin and Suzy – have you heard anything?"

"Things are bad – now the parents are into it," he said as he closed the folder. When he was deeply concerned, his brow wrinkled, and his eyes became a deeper blue. He took off his glasses and put them on the top of the folder.

"I'm afraid we're in for real trouble!"

Nodding in agreement, Mrs. A sat down and pulled a chair closer to the desk. She added, "The kids are afraid of what Suzy's father might do. Last week they told me he went to the Quarry and threatened Justin."

"Justin was in here Friday afternoon. He's been driving by the house, calling Suzy at all hours, and begging to see Billy. It's a mess!"

Mrs. Anderson had both of them in class together and remembered the afternoon they brought Billy in so she could see him. "They've been like a married couple for two years, Billy is his child, and this is like a nasty divorce. You just can't rip a kid from his father even if he's only a kid himself. Especially if he's only a kid himself. Something bad is going to happen!"

Nancy, Jim's secretary had arrived in the outer office and was hovering by the open office door. Probably some urgent paper work in the folder in her hand.

"Let's get them both in here- Period 3," he said looking at the schedule.

"That's your free period, right? Jenny nodded. I'll have someone pull them from Math class."

JUSTIN AND SUZY – PRODUCTS EIGHT AND NINE

Period three there were three chairs in front of the principal's desk. Justin was slumped over looking at the floor in the one on the right, Mrs. A. was sitting upright in the middle one and Suzy was sitting gingerly on the left hand side.

"So, what's going on?" Mr. McManus asked.

Suzy and Justin didn't take offence at his inquiry because he was the one who helped them when Suzy first found out she was pregnant, the one who had made it possible for her to be in school during a difficult pregnancy, and had arranged for a tutor to go to her house when she was so sick at the end. He was the one who allowed Justin to leave early this year in a Work Study Program to go to Simond's. McManus was a friend.

Justin Tobin was a husky, hard-working eighteen year old with black hair that never seemed combed. His plaid shirt was tucked into his jeans and his heavy boots were the kind all mechanics at Simond's wear. He twisted his hat with Deere written on the visor in his hands, looked at the beige squares on the floor and blurted out to the principal, "She says I can't see Billy!"

"I didn't say that." Suzy whispered. "He's my kid too."

"Don't you think I know that?" she said in a louder voice.

"Yeah, sure." Justin answered just to say something.

She shot back, "Then, what about supporting him if he's your kid?"

"Wait a minute! Didn't I give you every cent I earned?" "Not last week!"

"One week – Jesus, Suzy. That's your father talking!" "Leave my father out of this."

The voices of the two got louder and louder as they shot accusations and recriminations back and forth across the room for most of period 3. It was the wretched sound of two young people who were desperate at the thought of breaking up. They knew it hurt but just didn't know how to fix the pain.

Suzy, a cute well-liked senior, usually brightened the room with her smile. No smile today! Now, she sat straight with her back pressing hard against the back of the chair. The usual quick smile was gone and she refused to look at Justin. Her voice was tinged with resentment and hurt.

"You cheated on me." There was a long pause.

"After you threw me out," Justin muttered to the beige square tiles on the floor. Suzy heard it.

"You'll never see Billy again. My father will see to that."

In an unguarded moment of rage, Justin got up from his chair.

"I'll kill you, I'll kill you – If you think you can take Billy." He hit his fist on the back of the chair, then sat down again and burst into tears. Suzy looked out the window remembering what her father said about him being "no good" and that she and Billy could do better. Besides he went out with Brenda Sutton – that whore – Brenda.

A long silence. Mrs. Anderson knew she had to intervene. She pushed her chair back so that she could address them both.

"Wait a minute. I've watched you guys for two years and you've had some tough times but you've had a good relationship. And you both love Billy."

Jim McManus interjected, "Sometimes things get messed when the parents get involved because they are trying to protect you. But you are Billy's parents now and have to think of him."

Embarrassed to have cried in from of them, Justin rubbed the tears from his face with his hat. Suzy straightened her sweater folding it carefully in place. She pushed her hair back off her shoulders and glanced at her boyfriend.

"This is your relationship, not your parents," Mrs. A said as she moved closer to the center of the two. Now, Suzy was crying – her back slumped - no longer pressed to the back of the chair. Justin leaned towards her and touched her arm lightly.

"I'm sorry, Suzy, about Brenda. I know I messed up. But we didn't do nothing. I swear to God, nothing." Justin offered looking directly at Suzy.

Another silence. A strange calm filtered into the room. It was almost time for the bell. Mrs. A seized the moment.

"I don't know if you can work this out or not – you might not be able to - and I don't know what's right to do. But I don't think you should leave here without knowing something." Another silence. She took the chance!

"Justin, do you love Suzy?" A long silence.

"Yes."

Another short silence. "Suzy, do you love Justin?" Another long silence.

A whispered "yes."

"If that's all you can take from here – take this one moment and remember it. When you get so mad you can't stand it, remember this moment." The bell rang.

IN THE PRESENT

JUNE 10ᵀᴴ - GRADUATION DAY

JUST BEFORE THE GRADUATION CEREMONY - 5:45 PM - SUZY STEVENSON'S FAMILY ARRIVE WITH JUSTIN AND SUZY'S CHILD, BILLY

Suzy Stevenson's family arrived early pulling into the

back parking lot of the Town Hall. Ned Stevenson automatically claimed his spot under the sign that said, **RESERVED TOWN OFFICIAL**. For the last 15 years Ned had been the **TOWN CODE ENFORCEMENT OFFICER** and this was his spot during the work day. He came early so that no one would take his place tonight.

Ned was the first one to get out of the Explorer. A big man, Ned's bulky frame rose up six foot five inches – far taller than most men. His ideal weight was about 240 pounds and hard work and a healthy appetite helped him maintain that. He had a barrel-like chest with defined forearms and shoulders that looked like the melons he grew in his garden. His hands were big with long fingers and well kept nails. A band of black curly hair circled his balding head; his face was ruggedly square softened only by light blue eyes.

When Ned wasn't inspecting buildings in town, he worked for his brother driving a bull dozer. And when he wasn't driving the bull dozer, he was mowing the lawn, working in the garden, pruning the trees, or doing a little plumbing for friends and family.

"Hey, buddy, you ready to go? Your mommy and daddy - graduate," he said as he reached into the back of the Explorer. Billy who had just had his third birthday last week reached out his arms towards the light blue eyes.

"I see mommy and daddy."

"Yeah, graduate, Billy, high school."

"HI School." The child looked around to see who he needed to wave to. The grandfather laughed and hugged the little boy with a tenderness that belied his size.

"No, Billy we go to school."

"To School, Grampy, we go school."

Now out of the car, Eleanor, Ned's wife was fussing with her dress, smoothing it down over her hips and straightening the buttons on her jacket. One had come undone. She buttoned it. Elly was plump like a ripe tomato. When Ned hugged her he could feel softness all around. Her brown hair was always curled the same way. She had an equally soft face with a hint of a more youthful time of real beauty. Her trademark – green eyes and a mischievous smile. "Wait for me, you two," she said hustling along after them. "What's your hurry?"

"I want to sit on the side – just in case Billy gets to acting up." Ned explained. Elly just nodded her head and continued to hustle after the man and boy.

When Elly wasn't cooking for Ned, or cleaning the house, she was taking care of Billy. She figured Suzy and Justin needed to finish high school so she had Billy until about 3 every school day. Sometimes she complained about it to Ned but most of the time she had fun with Billy. They had their routine – breakfast, lunch and nap.

She left the kids alone at night unless they wanted to come over for dinner. Sometimes they ate over at Justine's house. They were talking about getting married and Ned had let up on Justin after Justin had that talk with him last winter. This spring, Justin helped set the plants in the garden and helped Ned change the sparkplugs in the Explorer.

"Grampy, this school?" "Not yet, Billy."

"Why, Grampy?"

"It's graduation, Billy." "Not school, Grampy?" "Not yet, Billy." "WHY?"

The grandfather gave up the circular questioning as he zeroed in on a whole row of seats at the back where the two families could sit together.

"How many Eleanor?"

"Joe and Betty, and Steven, Aunt Jane, and Gramma, Emil and Priscilla, and the Hogans – and us - that's 12."

Still carrying the inquisitive child in his arms, Ned flipped up the seats on nine extra chairs as he went over the names and numbers in his mind. **Justin's parents, Joe and Betty Tobin, and Steven, Justin's brother would sit beside them with little Billy.** That way they could pass him back and forth if he got rambunctious. The others, friends and relatives could sit closer to the middle aisle to take pictures of Suzy and Justine. Bill Hogan promised to bring his camcorder.

Later that evening, after the "Pomp and Circumstance" had been played, and the seniors in steely blue and white gowns had processed to the stage and Billy yelled out, "Mommy, I go to school," the diplomas were about to be given out.

Shielding her eyes from the sun, Suzy scanned the audience to find their parents. She spotted her father first with Billy asleep in his arms. Just like him to sleep through the whole thing she thought. Then, she saw her mother whispering something to Justin's mother. Betsy smiled. And there was Aunt Jane with "Gramma". The sun in her eyes, Suzy blinked back tears.

As Mr. McManus delivered his final speech to the graduating class, she remembered that day in his office and when they both answered "Yes" to the "I love you" question. In the seating line-up, Justin was in "t's" and she was in the "s's" – she stole a glance to her left. He looked up and mouthed, "I love you." And she "Me too'd" him back. Mr.

McManus noticed the communication, smiled, and then, concluded his speech, "I will always fondly remember this graduating class." A cheer erupted from the graduates. A helicopter flew overhead. Billy woke up.

"Life Star" Grampy whispered to Eleanor. "Twinkle, Twinkle, Little Star?" Billy said.

IN THE LIFE STAR HELICOPTER

"Her pressure's dropping. Let's get out of her." The IV tubes rubbed up against each other as the plane churned into the sky. The motion of the helicopter shook Jenny. She felt her body rise above the scene below. She watched the medical team inside the copter as they inserted a tube, her blood rushed out. It was as if her SPIRIT had become HER BODY. Then she heard:

"KIDS NEED SCHOOL ACTIVITIES TO RAISE SCHOOL SPIRIT. WE'LL HAVE A SPIRIT WEEK – A SCHOOL FACTORY ACTIVITY.

SPIRIT WEEK IS A SERIES OF DAYS THAT ARE SUPPOSED TO PICK UP THE DRAGGING SPIRITS OF THE PRODUCTS. ON MONDAY THE STUDENTS DRESS UP LIKE CLOWNS AND TUESDAY DO "DIFFERENT SEX" DRESSING AND WEDNESDAY IT'S "UNDERPANTS DAY" AND SO FORTH ALL WEEK.

FOR SOME STRANGE REASON **THE STUDENT COUNCIL**, WHICH IS A GROUP OF THE

MOST SPIRITED STUDENTS IN THE SCHOOL FACTORY, THINK THEY CAN GET THE OTHER KIDS – THE ONES THAT THEY SOMETIMES CALL **"DRUGGIES", "NERDS" "LONERS"** AND **"WORK STUDY KIDS"** - TO GET MORE SPIRITED BY CONVINCING THEM TO DRESS UP IN THESE TERRIBLE COSTUMES. THE **"JOCKS"** AND **"CHEERLEADERS"** WILL LEAD THE WAY.

SOME **ADVISOR TO THE STUDENT COUNCIL** SOMEPLACE IN THE MID-WEST WROTE AN ARTICLE IN THE **STUDENT COUNCIL NEWSLETTER** ABOUT SPIRIT WEEK SO IT SEEMED LIKE A GOOD IDEA.

OUR **STUDENT COUNCIL PRESIDENT** WHO IS THE MOST POPULAR, SPIRITED KID IN THE WHOLE SCHOOL DECIDED TO TRY IT. SHE PRESENTED THE IDEA FOR **A VOTE OF THE STUDENT COUNCIL** AND ALL HER FRIENDS EXUBERANTLY VOTED FOR IT BECAUSE THEY WANT TO BE HER FRIEND.

WHAT REALLY HAPPENS DURING SPIRIT WEEK IS THIS. THE **STUDENT COUNCIL OFFICERS** AND THE **"IN CROWD"**- THEIR FRIENDS, THE **POPULAR KIDS** LIKE THE **JOCKS** AND **CHEERLEADERS** - ALL DRESS UP IN **COSTUMES**. USUALLY, THEY HAVE THEIR PARENTS, BROTHERS OR SISTERS HELP THEM PULL IT ALL TOGETHER. THEY COME TO SCHOOL AND RUN AROUND FROM ONE **HOMEROOM** TO ANOTHER COUNTING THE KIDS WHO GET DRESSED UP. 3 FRESHMEN IN 03. 6 SOPHOMORES

IN 06. AND SO ON. THEY MAKE A LIST TO CALCULATE WHICH CLASS WINS EVERY DAY.

AT THE END OF THE WEEK, ALL THE KIDS MEET IN **THE GYMNASIUM FOR A "SPIRIT ASSEMBLY."** DURING THE ASSEMBLY, ALL THE KIDS PLAY GAMES, YELL AT EACH OTHER BY GRADE – AND THE CLASS THAT YELLS THE LOUDEST WINS. THAT IS THE GRAND CONCLUSION OF SPIRIT WEEK.

NO ONE EVER QUESTIONS WHY WE HAVE **SPIRIT WEEK** OR IF IT REALLY RAISES THE SPIRIT OF THE GENERAL POPULATION OF THE PRODUCTS AT THE SCHOOL FACTORY. THE KIDS WHO LIKE TO GET "HIGH" ON DRUGS OR ALCOHOL GET HIGH RIGHT BEFORE **THE ASSSEMBLY** BECAUSE THEY DON'T HAVE TO GO BACK TO CLASS. THEY REALLY DO A LOT OF YELLING, OR THEY DON'T SAY ANYTHING.

THE **NERDS** AND **LONERS** WON'T DRESS UP IN COSTUMES AND FEEL MORE ALONE THAN BEFORE AND **THE WORK STUDY KIDS** JUST LEAVE AT 1PM AND GO TO WORK RIGHT BEFORE THE ASSEMBLY.

NO ONE QUESTIONS IF THE **POPULAR STUDENT COUNCIL LEADERS**, THE **JOCKS**, AND THE **CHEERLEADERS,** WHO ARE RUNNING **SPIRIT WEEK** JUST GET MORE SPIRITED AND THE KIDS WHO REFUSE TO DRESS UP LIKE CLOWNS, OR WEAR UNDERWEAR, OR THE BOYS WHO REFUSE TO DRESS LIKE GIRLS, OR THE GIRLS WHO REFUSE TO DRESS LIKE BOYS, DON'T END UP **FEELING**

MORE DEPRESSED THAN THEY DID BEFORE. WE DON'T ASK TOO MANY QUESTIONS AT THE SCHOOL FACTORY, WE JUST DO THINGS – THINGS LIKE THEY DID LAST YEAR - OR SOMETHING LIKE THAT!

THE PAST JOURNEY

FEBRUARY 10ᵀᴴ – SKIPPING THE ASSEMBLY

It was the day of the Spirit Assembly so they decided to leave early and meet behind the shed at the end of the athletic field. Lots of kids would sneak out there for a smoke during school hours but no one was there at 1:15. Cigarette butts had been ground into the snow during the winter but now were sucked up in the brown mud after an early thaw. Jim leaned up against the shed and waited listening absently to the kids yelling in the gymnasium. At 1:16 Kurt showed up.

Affectionately, he pulled on the front of Jim's shirt. "Nice! Birthday present?"

"Yeah, from me to me."

"Those are the best ones." He said as he lit up a cigarette. The wind took the sparks from its tip and scattered them over the front of his jacket. He brushed them off in a quick jerky movement. Jim reached out to help.

"I did it." Kurt said with that child-like teasing voice that Jim had come to love. At first he didn't understand then he remembered that Kurt had been talking about "coming out" to his parents.

"No shit, you didn't. What happened?"

"It was after supper and it just happened. We were at the table and my mom was talking about prejudice against the blacks in town. You know how my parents are about prejudice."

"But what did you say?"

"I said I knew about prejudice – and we got into it. They wanted to know how I knew. Finally, I said I knew because I was gay."

"What did they say?"

"Just that they had suspected and were glad I could trust them." Kurt stomped one more cigarette butt into the mud.

"No shit, you came out to your parents, I can't believe it. I'll never tell my Dad. He already thinks I'm a loser. He'd have a breakdown."

"Jim, I told them about us."

"What?" Jim leaned hard against the wall pulling his arm over his distraught face. "But you said you wouldn't. Jesus, Kurt, how could you do that?"

"Don't worry. They would've figured it out any way. They're not stupid. They promised not to tell anyone. Said we could hang out at the house after school like we always do. Nothing's going to change."

Somehow, Jim knew that everything in his life had changed that day.

JIM -THE TENTH PRODUCT

Most of the kids, except some homophobic jocks, liked Jim and Kurt and accepted that they were gay. Kurt was an incredible artist and Jim, a gifted musician. Jim had played the violin since he was eight. Ken Stanton, the music teacher, said he was an unusually sensitive musician.

Since freshman year, Jim played first chair in the school orchestra, and Mr. Stanton tried to convince him he had a future in music. This year he got him applications for Julliard in New York and the Hartt School of Music in Hartford. Jim tucked the applications into his three ring binder marked "music." He knew he could never get his father to OK any School of Music, even Julliard, so he never even brought it up at home.

Chet Bartlett, Jim's father, was a burly man who hated his son's sensitivity and saw it as weakness. His music just made him more effeminate and "girly" in his eyes. When he was a kid, Chet tried to get Jim interested in the things he liked: all terrain vehicles, motorcycles and ski mobiles. Jim would accommodate his father for awhile but eventually he would always retreat to his room and get lost in his music.

Anita Bartlett's, Jim's mother, was generally mild mannered and never really defied Chet on any issue; but her father had been an accomplished pianist so she challenged her husband and fought for her son and his music.

Jim sat in the back of Mrs. Anderson's level one English class. He was a disciplined, hardworking student who never caused a problem. A very good looking boy, with dark curly hair, facial features that were distinct like the models in the Abercrombie catalog, and clear brown eyes that carried a knowing secret pain. He could easily be the teacher's favorite student.

At first, some of the girls took notice of him but eventually they found out that he hung out with Kurt all the time so they backed away. Except for Stacey, who was his special friend. They waited for each other after class and whispered to each other in a special way – the way of best buddies.

Mrs. Anderson knew that something was terribly wrong with Jim's home life on Parent's night when she couldn't make his father understand that Jim was a wonderful boy. The father seemed to be looking for defects and the mother stood silently by. It was as if the father was looking for someone to confirm his strong disapproval of his son.

Jim knew he would never be able to make his father understand him so he gave up and avoided him. It wasn't too difficult because his father drove a trailer truck and was gone most of the week. On the weekends, he would hang out with Kurt or retreat to his room.

After Kurt "outed" him, Jim felt betrayed and completely alone. It was a loneliness that turned into a pain that covered him like a blanket. Somehow, he couldn't escape.

Luckily, the week after Kurt told Jim about divulging their secret to his parents, a northeaster came in and Jim's father was stuck in upper state New York. He didn't have to deal with him. School was called off from Wednesday to Friday.

Jim slept late for two days but on Friday morning he managed to drag himself over to the last rehearsal before the big concert to be held that Sunday. It was the same Sunday every year and Mr. Stanton would never change it. During rehearsal, he kept messing up even as he played his favorite concerto. Kurt was on his mind. He couldn't concentrate. They hadn't spoken all week.

On Saturday night, Jim borrowed his mother's car to "go out for awhile – maybe over to Kurt's house". His mother thought he looked pale but she never thought to question her son.

"Be careful on the slippery roads and say 'Hi' to Kurt," she said quietly as she handed him the car keys that were always kept in the small basket on the table in the back hall. The light was dim, so she failed to notice her husband's gun had been removed from the gun case beside the back door.

BEYOND THE PRESENT

LOOKING DOWN ON THE GRADUATION

As the Life Star pulled away from the Graduation ceremony, Mrs. Anderson focused on the scene below. The graduates in bright blue and white were seated on the stage in front of the parents and friends. Mrs. A. saw her empty seat and wondered why she wasn't there.

Then, Mrs. A. felt someone touch her. It was Jim Bartlett's voice that spoke.

"Come with me. I'll show you the lesson." "But you are not supposed to be here." "Come with me, Mrs. A. It's a new place."

Now she was the student and he was the teacher. "Remember that week-end. The week-end before the school concert? Well, I knew I was in trouble and I was secretly hoping someone would be able to help me," Jim said. "Watch you'll see how I left my violin at the band rehearsal. I was trying to leave a clue. Mr. Stanton found it. And he might have stopped me but he didn't know I was in so much trouble."

Time and space joined together and Mrs. A. went back in her mind, which had expanded now to include all memories of all people, to watch the week-end unfold. She could see Ken as he left the school to visit his fiancé, Ellie.

"Do you think we should be watching them? How can we see the past? How can we remember his memories?" She questioned Jim. He silenced her.

The movie-like memory continued as they watched Jim and Ellie. They saw him kissing her goodbye - after skiing all day Saturday. They saw him leave Ellie's home to return to conduct the concert on Sunday. They watched as Mr. Stanton drove right by the ball field.

The scenes fit together like a movie.

"If I had turned to him when I needed him, he could have helped me. But I didn't because it wasn't meant to be." Jim said.

"If he had come to find you when he saw the violin case, you might have been saved. Is that the lesson?"

"No, we come into the world at exactly the right moment and we leave at exactly the right moment. Time blends into itself. No one is to blame. There is a perfect timing for all things. There are no beginnings or endings — time blends into itself. That is the lesson!"

For now, Jenny felt reluctant to accept this simple explanation but when she did the peacefulness of acceptance entered her being and transformed her. Then she understood!

THE PAST JOURNEY

FEBRUARY 17TH - AFTER THE REHEARSAL

After the rehearsal, while Ken Stanton was packing the music stands and boxes of sheet music into his Subaru, he noticed a violin case in the corner. He checked the case for a name.

"Yeah, it's Jim's. Wonder if he's alright. Seemed distracted – kept losing his place. He never does that. Hope I wasn't too hard on him. I'll have to call him tonight." He said to the empty room. Jim's violin was the last thing he loaded into the van.

On his way to Killington to spend the night with his fiancée, Ellie, Ken ran into some intermittent snow squalls and hit a few icy patches on the road. The music stand and boxes of sheet music shifted uneasily in the back of the SUV. Jim's violin case teetered precariously on the back seat. Ken reached over and put it down securely on the floor in the front of the van. Then, his thoughts turned to Ellie. Tonight before it got dark, he would stack the wood under the car port while she made supper. Tomorrow they would ski all day at Killington.

It was nearly five o'clock when Ken pulled into Coburn Woods. The snow was falling steadily now. Ellie's condo was part of a group of a free standing homes nestled comfortably at the bottom of the mountain. Coburn Woods always made him feel like he was home.

Inside Ellie made a salad as the beef stew was cooking in the crock-pot. An apple pie was baking in the oven.

"Smells good," he said as he tripped over the sill

pushing his bulky six foot plus frame into the room. The snow fell from his shoulders and arms. Ken was completely unaware of his commanding physical presence. What he didn't know was that at 32 years old, he was the secret love of many girls at Heritage High. They saw his blond hair and blue eyes and noticed a sensual boyishness that emerged when he conducted the orchestra. Unaware of the admiration, Ellie was his only love. They had been together for three years and would be married next June.

She kissed him and he kissed her back. When she tried to pull his ski jacket from his shoulders, he resisted.

"We'll finish this later," he said kissing her again. "I better stack the wood while I still have some light."

After dinner, they decided to "try out the wood" and made a roaring fire in the fireplace. The snow gently drifted into Coburn Woods that night.

FEBRUARY 18ᵀᴴ - COMING HOME FOR THE CONCERT

The next day Ellie and Ken skied all day. The cold air stung their faces and numbed their hands but they attacked the slopes long into the afternoon. They savored the cold air much as they relished the warmth of the fire the night before.

"Do you have to go back tonight?" Ellie said as they finished their last run. She didn't wait for an answer because she knew he would have to leave tonight to get ready for Sunday's concert. Later, Ken kissed her good-bye as they lingered at the door.

It wasn't until he had waved goodbye for a second time and made the turn out of Coburn Woods that he noticed Jim's violin.

"Damn, I forgot to call him," he said as he reached for his cell phone. Maneuvering the cell phone and the icy roads became a challenge so he pulled over. He heard a deep voice say, "Chet Bartlett here. Leave a message."

"Uhh, yes, Jim. This is Ken Stanton. You left your violin at school. I, I have it in my car and I'll bring it to the concert. See you tomorrow."

It was nearly ten o'clock when Ken came to the rotary near the end of RT 3. He saw a police car turning toward the high school. The Heritage Police were on a routine check behind the school when they saw a car pulled up behind the shed near the football field. They put a light on it.

"Probably a couple of kids making out," Larsen said to Hennessey, his partner.

"Or, drunk," Hennessey shot back. "Seems like a strange place to be parked though. We'd better call it in."

The radio crackled as he picked it up. "We have a car parked near the shed, right behind the goal post on the football field, Heritage High," he told the dispatcher. When Larsen and Hennessey got closer, they noticed someone slumped over the wheel.

"We got a drunk," Larsen said.

The light from his flashlight in front of him, Hennessey approached the car. The slumped figure didn't move. Hennessey pushed the light up to the window making out the outline of a boy slumped over the wheel. "We definitely got a drunk, dead drunk!"

Larsen followed with his light. No one moved. He pointed the light shaft into the back seat expecting to see beer cans on the floor. Instead he saw fresh blood stains, rivulets of blood that had seeped down between the seat and gathered into a bright red pool on the floor.

"Jesus, this kid's been shot."

The next day, Jim never showed up to play the Mozart concerto solo. Expecting him to walk in at the last minute, Ken left his seat empty. Then at the last minute he changed the arrangement.

"Play Jim's part," he said to Hilda, the second chair.

Right after the concert, when Ken called Jim's house, a family friend who was answering the phone for Mrs. Bartlett, told him Jim was dead. Committed suicide - last night around ten o'clock - over at the high school — behind the shed.

BEYOND THE PRESENT

LOOKING DOWN FROM ABOVE

When Jenny's heart stopped, she felt herself rise above the scene below. Jim Bartlett joined her and communicated with her. His presence drew her attention away from what was happening in the Life Star Helicopter. But she was still curious about her body.

She watched without alarm as the medical team started the defibrillation process — counting - one- two- three — pause - hit and count again! But her spirit continued to fly free of her body — so all she could do was watch with a disassociated, curious interest.

She wondered why she was "absent" from her body. She knew she had to be absent! The VOICE of EDUCATION TALKED about EXCESSIVE

ABSENTEEISM and the need for A NEW ATTENDANCE POLICY for the SCHOOL FACTORY.

"A NEW ASSISTANT FOREMAN CAME TO THE SCHOOL FACTORY TO INSTITUTE **A NEW ATTENDANCE POLICY**. TOO MANY KIDS WERE SKIPPING SCHOOL AND FAILING CLASSES. WE ALL KNOW YOU CAN'T PROGRESS DOWN THE CONVEYOR BELT OF EDUCATION IF YOU'RE NOT EVEN ON THE CONVEYOR BELT; BUT THEN, OF COURSE, YOU NEED TO ALLOW SOME KID'S TO STAY HOME WHEN THEY'RE SICK. SO, THE NEW ASSISTANT TOLD THE TEACHER WORKERS TO KEEP **A GREEN ATTENDANCE BOOK**. THERE WOULD BE **EXCUSED ABSENSES** AND **UNEXCUSED ABSENSES KEPT** IN THE BOOK. EVERY DAY, IN EVERY CLASS, THE TEACHER WOULD MARK DOWN **<u>A</u> FOR JUST PLAIN <u>ABSENT</u>, <u>A/S</u> FOR SCHOOL ABSENT LIKE A FIELD TRIP, <u>A/E</u> FOR <u>ABSENT EXCUSED</u> LIKE A DOCTOR'S VISIT,** THEN THERE WAS A **CIRCLED A THAT NO ONE QUITE UNDERSTOOD**.

SOME PARENTS COMPLAINED WHEN THE SCHOOL FACTORY DIDN'T HAVE AN ATTENDANCE POLICY BECAUSE THEIR KIDS WERE SKIPPING SCHOOL AND FLUNKING WITHOUT THEIR KNOWLEDGE.

TO MAKE THE ATTENDANCE POLICY WORK, THE TEACHER **HAD TO RECORD THE A'S, A/E'S, A/S'S AND CIRCLED A'S IN THE GREEN BOOK**. THEN THEY DILIGENTLY COUNTED THE ABSENCES AND SENT A FORM TO THE PARENTS AT

5 ABSENCES, 9 ABSENSES, AND 11 ABSENSES. AT 11 ABSENSES A DIFFERENT FORM HAD TO BE MADE OUT THAN THE 9 ABSENCES FORM: THIS WAS **A FINAL WARNING FORM. FIFTEEN UNEXCUSED ABSENCES IN THE SEMESTER MEANS YOU FAIL FOR THE YEAR!**

IF THE TEACHER MAKES A MISTAKE IN THE COUNTING OF ABSENCES, THE SECRETARY FOR THE NEW ASSISTANT FORMAN WILL NOTIFY THE TEACHER TO CHECK THE DATA AND SUBMIT A LIST OF THE A'S, A/E'S, A/S'S AND CIRCILED A'S. FOR THE KID WHO IS SKIPPING SCHOOL. THE TEACHER WILL HAVE TO STOP TEACHING THE PRODUCTS TO CHECK THE A'S, A/E'S, A/S'S AND CIRCLED A'S AND SEND THE REPORT BACK TO THE SECRETARY WHO GIVES IT TO THE NEW ASSISTANT FORMAN.

AFTER THE PARENTS GET THE FORM WITH THE EXACT DAYS LISTED ON IT AND CHECKED BY THE ASSISTANT FORMAN, THEY GET INVITED TO **A HEARING BEFORE THE ATTENDANCE COMMITTEE.** THE ATTENDANCE COMMITTEE IS MADE UP OF TEACHERS WHO MEET ON FRIDAYS FROM 2:30 TO 5:30.

AFTER A LONG HEARING WITH THE PARENTS, THE TEACHER, THE PRINCIPAL AND THE COMMITTEE OF TEACHERS, THE PARENTS USUALLY ARGUE THAT THEIR CHILD HAS HAD "A CHRONIC AND PROLONGED ILLNESS" AND PRODUCE A DOCTOR'S NOTE. **LOSS OF CREDIT** IS USUALLY RESTORED UNLESS THE PARENTS WERE

UNABLE TO FIND A DOCTOR TO WRITE THE NOTE.

THE SCHOOL FACTORY IS SUPPOSED TO HAVE A COMPUTERIZED SYSTEM FOR ATTENDANCE BUT IT'S NOT ACCURATE SO YOU CAN'T HAVE AN **ATTENDANCE POLICY** WITHOUT THE TEACHERS, THE GREEN BOOK, AND THE A'S, A/E'S,A/S'S AND THE CIRCLED A'S THAT NO ONE UNDERSTANDS.

ONE OF THE TIMES WHEN THE ATTENDANCE POLICY IS NOT IN EFFECT IS WHEN THERE IS A DEATH OF A STUDENT. **THE ASSEMBLY LINE SHUTS DOWN** FOR THESE **AUTHORIZED ABSENCES.**

WE HAD THREE DEATHS AT THE SCHOOL FACTORY THIS YEAR. EARLIER IN THE YEAR, TWO POPULAR GIRLS, SARAH AND MATTY, BOTH 16 YEARS OLD, WERE OUT DRIVING ONE NIGHT AND RAN INTO A TREE. SARAH ONLY HAD HER LICENSE FOR A FEW WEEKS AND IT APPEARS SHE HIT THE TREE BECAUSE SHE WAS GOING TOO FAST OR JUST DIDN'T TAKE ENOUGH **DRIVER EDUCATION CLASSES.**

LATER IN THE YEAR, WHEN JIM COMMITTED **SUICIDE OUT** NEAR THE SHED ON THE FOOTBALL FIELD. YOU KNOW, THE SHED WHERE THE KIDS SNEAK A CIGARETTE. WELL, THE ASSISTANT SCHOOL PRINCIPAL SAID THAT THE KIDS COULD TAKE **AN EXCUSED ABSENCE** TO GO TO HIS FUNERAL."

THE PAST JOURNEY

FEBRUARY 25TH - TAYLOR'S FUNERAL HOME

The Bartlett's decided to hold the memorial at Taylor's Funeral Home in the center of Heritage near the First Congregational Church. The minister would come to deliver the eulogy on Friday at 10 o'clock. Students were allowed an authorized absence from school. The parents thought a few of Jim's friends would stop by but never expected the outpouring of love and concern they experienced.

About nine-thirty, groups of kids began to gather in front of Taylor's. Mr. and Mrs. Bartlett waited by the casket. The room was crowded with relatives and friends. Mrs. Bartlett's mother consoled her daughter, Anita. Chet Bartlett stood awkwardly to the side.

Then, the students began to file in. The line moved slowly; there was no sound except muffled sobs. Some students cried because they realized that Jim was lonely and they hadn't reached out, some cried because they too had considered suicide, some cried remembering the terrible pain of Sarah and Matty's recent death. The moved like a gentle ocean wave healing the pain with their tears.

Kurt came with his parents and stood beside Jim's mother. The student's hugged him knowing of his love for Jim but never being able to mention it.

Kurt tried to help Mrs. Bartlett's, "This is Marylee Ames; she was in Jim's science class. Marylee hugged her. 'I'm so sorry'." The tears again. Marylee was Sarah's sister. She hurried along.

"Mrs. Anderson, Jim's English teacher."

"I know, thank you for coming. Jim always liked you –

he said you were fair to everyone."

"He was a wonderful boy – a pleasure to have in class. I'm so sorry." As Jenny Anderson looked at the closed casket and viewed the school picture of Jim, she realized that an entire lifetime was wasted in one desperate moment. She wished she had approached Jim when she saw his sadness.

One by one, Kurt made the connection between Jim and the mourners. Kurt's parents stood by his side introducing the parents that they knew. Chet Bartlett hung awkwardly by the door to the adjacent sitting room.

When Ken Stanton came, the line still reached out of Taylor's and spilled down the sidewalk. The music director waited on the side to join up with Hilda, his second violinist, and several other members of the ensemble chosen to play at the memorial. They gathered and entered through the back door.

When Steven Adams, the minister from the First Congregational Church finished the prayers, Mr. Stanton came forward. Mrs. Bartlett broke down when she saw Ken approaching because she knew he had encouraged and appreciated Jim like no one else. When she recognized the orchestra members with their instruments, she realized her loss even more. Jim would never play again!

Ken spoke briefly of Jim's talent and conducted a musical tribute to him explaining the significance of each song. Kurt stood tall and straight, head held high with quiet tears visible now. He wiped them away as they appeared. Chet Bartlett disappeared from the adjacent room as it filled with more students and parents.

Alex Brady and some others kids left the funeral home right after the musical tribute ended - just as the violin and cello's sweet sounds faded away. Alex was one of the few "straight" guys who befriended Jim. Sometimes they sneaked behind the shed for a smoke before class. It never mattered that Jim was gay. Other kids, like some of the jocks, or "wannabee jocks", made fun of him, and of Kurt, but Alex understood and respected him and his art, the musician in him. After all, Alex felt like he was outside the jock, cheerleader group too. Tonight he felt really bad – so he and some friends got "roaring" drunk.

THE VOICE OF EDUCATION SPOKE OUT AGAIN BUT NO ONE WAS THERE TO HEAR HIM:

"WHAT ABOUT DEFECTIVE PRODUCTS? – NOT ALL PRODUCTS COME DOWN THE ASSSEMBLY LINE IN THE SAME CONDITION. SOME ARE ALREADY DEFECTIVE. THE SCHOOL FACTORY DOESN'T KNOW WHAT TO DO FOR PRODUCTS THAT CAN'T BE EDUCATED.

WE DON'T HAVE A REJECT BIN OR DEFECTIVE TRACT FOR THE **"DRUGGIES"**, **"POT HEADS"** OR JUST PLAIN **"ALCOHOLICS".** ONE OUT OF TEN STUDENTS HAS THESE DAMAGING MALADIES.

IT HAPPENS IN EVERY HIGH SCHOOL IN AMERICA. NO AMOUNT OF **DRUG EDUCATION OR "JUST SAY NO PROGRAM"** CAN STOP IT. THE DEFECTIVE PRODUCTS SHOW UP IN EVERY CLASS – **ONE OUT OF TEN.**

THERE IS A KID NAMED ALEX WHOSE MOTHER WORKS IN THE TOWN HALL. WHEN HE IS

TOO **"SPACED OUT"**, **"DRUGGED UP"**, OR **"HUNG OVER"** HE LIES OR CHEATS. LAST YEAR, HE WAS CAUGHT TAKING AN EXAM FROM A TEACHER'S FILE CABINET. THE PRINCIPAL TALKED TO ALEX'S MOTHER BUT SHE REALLY DIDN'T THINK ALEX HAD A PROBLEM! HE HAS BEEN HYPERACTIVE ALL HIS LIFE AND HAD MORE PROBLEMS THAT OTHER KIDS.

ALL THE OTHER KIDS KNOW THAT ALEX DRINKS TO GET DRUNK – EVERY TIME HE DRINKS. JUST ASK NELLY ABOUT LAST SATURDAY NIGHT DOWN AT THE SAND PIT WHEN HE **"BLACKED OUT"** AND CALLED HER A "WHORE". OF COURSE, HE COULDN'T REMEMBER THE NEXT DAY. ALL THE KID'S KNOW WHAT ALEX'S MOTHER REFUSES TO SEE – THAT ALEX IS DRINKING EVERYDAY AND IS IN THE LAST STAGES OF ALCOHOLISM. HE'S JUST RIDING ON THE EDGE TRYING TO GET TO GRADUATION ANY WAY HE CAN.

EVERYONE KNOWS ALEX SHOULD BE TAKEN OUT OF THE SCHOOL FACTORY AND **SHIPPED TO A PLACE CALLED "REHAB"** WHERE THEY TRY TO FIX ALCOHOLIC PRODUCTS. THEY **DRY THEM OUT AND TEACH THEM TO STAY SOBER**. NO ONE AT THE SCHOOL FACTORY CAN HELP BECAUSE HIS MOTHER PROTECTS HIM ALLOWING HIM TO RIDE THE EDGE OF THE CONVEYOR BELT TO GRADUATION.

IF THE PRINCIPAL WERE TO STOP THE ASSEMBLY LINE AND **TAKE 10% OF THE PRODUCTS OFF THE LINE** AND SAY "THESE

PRODUCTS ARE DEFECTIVE," THE PARENTS WOULD INSTITUTE A **LAW SUIT** AGAINST THE SCHOOL PRINCIPAL AND THE SCHOOL DISTRICT. THE PUBLIC WOULD COMPLAIN TO THE SUPERINTENDENT AND THE SUPERINTENDENT WOULD TALK TO THE PRINCIPAL AND MAKE HIM CHANGE HIS DECISION."

THE PAST JOURNEY

MARCH 10TH–PREPARING FOR THE PPT MEETING FOR ALEX - ROOM 02 - LUNCHTIME

Mrs. Anderson almost forgot the PPT meeting scheduled for that afternoon. Priscilla, the quiet one from **SPECIAL EDUCATION** showed up in her room just as she was about to eat her lunch.

"Alex's PPT is this afternoon." She said with an ever so sweet tone laced with a faint hint of authority. A pretty girl, about twenty-two, fresh out of college, she never spoke above a whisper and apologized profusely when she didn't need to.

"Sorry to interrupt you." She offered as she took two bold steps into the room. Mrs. A. put down her sandwich. Priscilla auburn hair was neatly tied back with a barrette, her dress uncommonly short for a teacher. Mrs. A. looked at the clock and decided to finish her tuna sandwich while Priscilla talked.

"It's for Alex - at 3:30." "OK I'll be there."

Another hesitant question, "How's he doing?" Jenny Anderson picked up her green mark book and flipped to Period 5. How could she possibly explain to a Special

Education teacher that Alex had a 50 average because he was lazy, or sometimes too hung over to do the work? He had 30 absences from class and had been in class only half the time.

Trying to remain diplomatic, Mrs. A. wearily offered, "It's a bad situation. He really has to buckle down if he is going to pass for the year." She hesitated, too tired to get into it. The half corrected papers from her AP class were strewn out on the desk.

"Pass for the year!" That was all Priscilla could latch onto – the possibility that Alex might have a chance to pass for the year. She would address all her comments to the PPT Group this afternoon with these words. "If Alex is going to pass for the year, he has to:"

1. Complete assigned work and extra credit

2. Meet standards and requirements for the course

3. Comply with the attendance policy

4. Work things out with Mrs. Anderson who will be available to help him in any way she can.

ALEX – THE ELEVENTH PRODUCT

Alex is in the last stages of alcohol and drug addiction. He hates school and spends most of his time playing in a band. Every week the group plays at a different bar in Heritage or some surrounding town. What the group gets paid barely pays for the expenses of the band. A better guitar, sound equipment, Alex's old van that's always breaking down – and of course a few beers to get buzzed. Some time there's enough for some "coke."

In the fifth grade, Alex mother who was alarmed at Alex's grades decided to have him tested for a "learning disability". He was hyperactive and couldn't focus in class.

Somehow he kept disturbing the class by insisting that he get his own way. At home, he was allowed to do exactly whatever he wanted. He mother felt sorry for him, was overindulgent and incapable of any consistent discipline. His father was content with a six pack of beer a night and left the kids to his wife.

Alex was put on pills that helped him calm down in school and not disturb the class. It's logical that if he was using "mind altering drugs" in the fifth grade that when he turned 15, he would find more mind altering substances – like alcohol, weed and cocaine.

Alex had been tested, labeled, and put in a special small class with Priscilla, the Special Education teacher who monitored his **INTEGRATION INTO THE REGULAR CURRICULUM.** To satisfy the law and Alex's parents, regular PPT meetings would be held to monitor Alex's progress. No one spoke of Alex's progression into addiction.

AT 3:30 - THE PPT MEETING FOR ALEX

Gina Watson, THE SPECIAL EDUCATION DIRECTOR, was sitting at the head of the table in the conference room. Gina was a heavy set woman with dark glasses and mannerisms as precise as a head-chopping guillotine. Jenny Anderson needed to finish those AP essays so she arrived a bit late - at exactly 3:36. She took her seat at the end of the table.

"Now that Mrs. Anderson has joined us we can begin our assessment of Alex Brady." As she said Alex's name, she nodded towards him and his parents.

Alex who was sitting across from Mrs. A. gave her a

quick look that said, "This is all bull shit and we both know it."

To correct the "bad situation" Alex "HAPPENS TO FIND HIMSELF IN," we now had three members of the TEACHING STAFF and two SPECIAL EDUCATION DEPARTMENT MEMBERS, THE PRINCIPAL, THE GUIDANCE COUNSELOR, and the PARENTS all gathered together on this Friday afternoon in March. Combined salary base of these professionals was nearly 370,000 dollars plus the lost pay of both parents for the day.

The meeting begins!

Alex fiddles on the desk beating out the rhythm to a new song that he will play tonight. Wish I had a beer he thinks as he looks at the clock. He shuts out the sound of Gina and Priscilla as they talk about educational standards, attendance policy and completing assigned work. He half listened to Mr. McManus when he brings out the attendance book – 30 absences – that must be wrong!

Alex's mother speaks up. "Alex was very sick in November and December. He had the flu. We can get a doctor's slip," she said confidently knowing her brother-in- law is the family's primary care physician.

The truth is Alex is sick all the time. He stays out late three or four nights a week, gets high most nights, and is too tired to get up for school. Since he lives in the basement of his parent's ranch house, they really don't see him come in. There's a special entrance for Alex at the back of the house and a room where the band can rehearse in the garage. When Alex gets to school he cons the school nurse to let him rest in the nurse's office or gets an excuse from class from the school psychologist.

The truth is Alex doesn't think about school too much because he doesn't have to. Everyone thinks about school for him. During the meeting everyone except Mrs. Anderson talked about Alex in front of him while he was playing his music in his head. They were playing their parts in his "bad situation". Finally, Mr. McManus, who knew the real problem, had had enough.

"What about your drinking, Alex?" he blurted out. Alex began to listen. "There have been some mornings you've come into the front office in rough shape. Late for school! Hung over!" Mr. and Mrs. Brady leaned heavily into the conversation.

The mother led the way. "But we tell him he can't drink on week nights. That's the rule."

"We take the car when he comes home a little 'tipsy'," the father said.

The principal countered by looking directly at the boy who was finally paying attention. "Do you think you might have a problem with drinking, Alex?"

"No, I have a couple of beers on the week-ends — that's the extent of it! I just need to get here and do my work. I haven't been motivated. I'll have to try to do better."

The PARENTS glared at the PRINCIPAL and he retreated from the word "alcoholic" but that word was screaming to get out of his mouth.

Finally, it was the moment she was waiting for. Mrs. Anderson took out her green mark book and looked at the 50 percent beside Alex's name, waited a second and flipped to the attendance sheets at the back of the book. She counted the absences at over 30.

"It looks pretty bad here. You'll need an A average for

the rest of the year to get a 65. That means no missed assignments, no missed days, make-up tests for this term, extra credit assignments each week and homework done on time. From what I've seen so far this year, that's just not going to happen!"

"Yeah." He slumped in his seat.

"What are you going to do Alex? Do you want to graduate?"

A sharp voice interrupted their conversation. Mrs. A. swung in the direction of that voice and gestured it away, "No, No! I want to hear from Alex! Almost everyone in the room has talked about Alex in front of Alex, I am speaking to Alex!"

"What are you going to do?" she insisted.

"Well, I can't miss anymore days. If I don't miss anymore, the attendance committee might take my medical excuse. If they don't, I can appeal it. I'd have to read the two books you gave us and pass those tests. Write those papers for those books and do the work for the rest of the year. Maybe you could give me extra credit for the songs I write – like a poetry notebook grade."

"I could do that. But can you do all the rest?" "I could try", he hesitated.

"Trying is lying, Alex. And trying hasn't worked for you so far."

"Can you do all that to get your average up to 65?" she persisted.

"I can do it! I want to graduate!' Alex settled back in his seat and for the first time stopped thinking about getting home to have a beer. He knew Mrs. A. would flunk him if he didn't do the work. This time he had no excuse, no one to answer the questions for him.

Soon after Mrs. Anderson and Alex had their conversation, everyone scribbled down some notes, picked up and went home - leaving the real work to Mrs. A and Alex. The **SPECIAL EDUCATION DIRECTOR** was satisfied to have conducted another successful PPT for the year. She would write it up as:

Alex Brady's Educational Plan

1. Meet standards and requirements for the Course
2. Complete assigned work and extra credit
3. Comply with Attendance Policy
4. Work things out with teacher who will be available to help Michael in any way possible.

On the ride home, Mr. and Mrs. Brady talked about McManus and how he insulted Alex, practically calling him an alcoholic. They just knew he had it in for their son. They said Mrs. Anderson would have to pass him now because the SPECIAL EDUCATION DIRECTOR would be checking up on her. They were relieved because now Alex had a chance to graduate.

Bill Brady stopped at the village "packy" to pick up his "Bud" for the night. Mrs. Brady couldn't wait to call her sister to tell her the great news.

That night Alex drove the car that had been "taken away for one week" to his friend Danny's house. Danny's mother died of cancer last year and his father worked the night shift.

"I <u>have</u> to do the work, Dan. She'll nail me!" he told his friend as he popped a Miller Lite.

After awhile Dan rummaged through his desk drawer

and came up with two tests from Mrs. A's class. He'd heard she <u>never</u> gives the same test twice but you might get lucky.

Thanks to his buddy, Alex felt relieved and was sure he was on the right track. They finished off the six pack and smoked a little weed. It was almost 1 AM when Alex quietly sneaked through the cellar door into his room in the basement.

For the next two months Alex showed up in class every day. He started to make up the missed assignment, read the books, passed the tests with an 89 and 92, and turned in an extra credit project of songs he had been composing. He even got to share his work with the class in an oral report. The class was impressed. Things looked better for Alex.

Then one night, before he played a gig in Rutland, he got "a little hammered." At about midnight, there was a fight when one of the guys hit on Alex's girlfriend. There were a few punches thrown, Alex staggered, the guy hit him squarely on the chin and knocked him down. The other band members stopped the fight and helped Sandy, Alex's girl, get him home. They dumped him off at his house without waking the Bradys. The next morning, Alex woke up with a terrible pain in his jaw but couldn't remember much of the night before because he had blacked out.

It was about a month until graduation. When Alex was late for class, Mrs. Anderson was about to mark him absent when he came flying through the door. He looked terrible! One day absent and I'm done he thought. No graduation! I have to do this.

For about twenty-five minutes he stayed in his seat holding back tears from the excruciating pain. Then, finally he came to the front desk and said, "I need to go to the nurse." At first, Mrs. A. hesitated asking him to stay five more minutes.

But then she realized that his pain was real. His face was twisted and pale.

Alex had a fractured jaw. No more drinking for six weeks, no more singing with the band, no more talking, or much of anything. After that Alex came to class every day with his jaw wired shut. In a note to Mrs. A., he confided he had stopped drinking and he and Sandy were "going to meetings".

Week by week his face brightened, his eyes cleared and he seemed to have hope for the first time. In those weeks, Jenny Anderson grew fond of Alex and admired his tenacity – sitting there every day with his jaw wired shut! He could have had a medically excused absence but he refused it. He never missed a day and did all his work. When she averaged out his grades for the year, his earlier zeros drove down his average to 64.5. Technically he needed a 65. She gave him his first A in English that term, rounded up his average to 65

- and sent his name to the Principal for THE GRADUATION LIST.

ONCE AGAIN THE VOICE OF EDUCATION INTERRUPTED IN A LOUD VOICE BUT NO ONE SEEMED TO HEAR.

"LAST YEAR, THE SCHOOL DEPARTMENT NEEDED TO ACCEPT TUITION STUDENTS TO HELP DEFRAY THE COST OF RUNNING THE SCHOOL. THE TOWNSPEOPLE WERE GETTING A HERITAGE HIGH NEWSLETTER FROM THE SUPERINTENDENT. THEY WERE TOLD EVERYTHING IS FINE AT THE SCHOOL FACTORY.

THE TOWN TAKES IN 150 TUITION STUDENTS @ 7,000 DOLLARS FOR EACH STUDENT FROM THE STATE OF VERMONT. THAT ADDS ONE MILLION AND FIFTY THOUSAND DOLLARS TO THE SCHOOL BUDGET. BUT THE TEACHERS CAN'T POSSIBLE RUN THAT MANY PRODUCTS THROUGH THE ASSEMBLY LINE AND CREATE EDUCATED PRODUCTS. MOST OF THE TOWN DOESN'T CARE BECAUSE THEY HAVE FOUND A WAY TO KEEP THEIR TAXES FROM GOING UP.

SOME "DEDICATED" TEACHERS STILL BELIEVE THEY CAN FIND <u>5 MINUTES EACH WEEK</u> TO CORRECT EACH PRODUCT'S PAPERS. FOR 130 STUDENTS, THAT IS, AN EXTRA TEN HOURS OF CORRECTING AT HOME EACH WEEK. TWO HOURS, MONDAY – TWO HOURS, TUESDAY- TWO HOURS, WEDNESDAY – TWO HOURS, THURSDAY – TWO HOURS, ON THE WEEK-END.

TEACHERS ARE WEARING OUT FROM THE WORK LOAD, WITH A DISEASE CALLED BURN-OUT. SOME USE SICK DAYS JUST TO SURVIVE. SOME LEAVE OR RETIRE IF THEY CAN. CLASSES ARE BECOMING UNMANAGEABLE; KIDS ARE FALLING OFF THE ASSEMBLY LINE AS DROP OUTS. THE TEACHER'S UNION THREATENS TO STRIKE AND STOP THE ASSEMBLY LINE ALTOGETHER.

THE PUBLIC IS ENRAGED THAT THEIR TEACHERS WOULD COMPLAIN. THE PRODUCTS KEEP GETTING PUSHED INTO A SMALLER

SPACE ON THE CONVEYOR BELT. LESS BOOKS, MORE DESKS IN THE ROOM. MANY JUST SLIP OFF AND NEVER GET EDUCATED."

BEYOND THE PRESENT

TIMELESSNESS ABOVE THE GRADUATION

Jim continued to teach Mrs. A. "In spirit there is no time. No boundaries. Just timelessness," he said.

"Timelessness?" she questioned.

"Think of it this way. Now you have a spiritual tool, a mental remote control that allows you to fast forward or replay time. Just think of someone."

Mrs. Anderson thought of Ryan, one of the tuition students who was in trouble with the law, and fast forwarded to a maximum security prison in Tallahassee. A strong sense of despair went through her spirit. His parents no longer visited him and his main concern was to work on his parole papers. She saw him alone in his cell with the papers spread out on the floor before him. She paused her thoughts because it was too painful.

Time switched to the spring when Ryan was partying and selling drugs. She saw it all.

THE PAST JOURNEY
MARCH 17TH – ST. PATRICK'S DAY - PARTYING

AT THE SAND PIT

The dirt road into the sand pit was just thawing out. Some of the ruts were still capped with ice and oozing with brown mud but Ryan knew he had to push on. Under the back seat of his Jeep was a stash of weed and pills that he had to unload.

"One thing there ain't no cops out here."

"Not yet, anyway," said Jason as he struggles to hang onto the handle on the side of the door. He remembered last summer when Larson and that other Heritage cop came out here. Good thing Ryan didn't have any stuff that night. Lucky bastard, Ryan's always lucky he thought.

"We're good," Ryan said as he saw the bonfire raging in the center of the fire ring. Several trucks were parked in a semicircle around the fire. Then, Jake who recognized the jeep came towards them. He had a Millers in one hand and a cigarette in the other. He waved them in.

Ryan had just come back to Heritage High this year. He had been in some trouble. Word spread pretty quick that you could get "anything" you might need from Ryan.

So, after awhile the kids who wanted some "stuff" gathered over by the Jeep as Ryan emptied out the back seat. Most kids just got a "nickel bag" but some got into fancier stuff. It all depended on how much money they could put together. Ryan stuffed the money under the front seat in a special box – the one that had the small hand gun in it. Everyone knew that they couldn't mess with Ryan. He stayed close to the Jeep having a beer with Jason and Jake.

"Just one - for Saint Patty's day," he chuckled - all the while nervously watching the front seat of the Jeep. Pretty soon, he and Jason headed back down the rut filled dirt road they had come in on.

Ever since Matty and Sarah died and Jim killed himself, the kids have been getting together "Saturday Nites at the Pits." They would talk, drink, and smoke cigarettes and some "weed," as they hovered around the fire. It was mostly guys, a couple of couples, and three or four girls hanging together.

Harry couldn't hold his booze so he usually got plastered. Sometimes he was hammered by the time he got there. He would say some awful things to the girls when he was loaded. The guys would argue and sometimes a fight broke out. The couples usually left early because the girls didn't like it when the "name-calling" and fighting started.

Jake could "hold his liquor" and keep a cool head. He usually put the fire out and told the last few stragglers to go home. All of the parents didn't know where their kids were on Saturday nights. The kids always lied! The guys would say they were going to someone's house to work on their truck, or just out riding around; the girls would say they were going to a movie or the mall.

Sometimes they had a designated driver, but most of the time they'd just pick the least "messed up" kid to drive home. When their parents asked "Who was with you?" they would usually cover for each other.

Most of the time the kids came to the sand pit because it was the only place they could come to be together. They talked about school, the teachers, their parents, and the snotty kids who think they're so special. The ones who would never be seen dead at the sand pit! The sand pit was a place where they could belong.

RYAN – THE TWELVTH PRODUCT

When he was 15 years old, Ryan Blakely had been expelled from a private school because he blew up a stink bomb in the boy's bathroom. He thought it was funny. So did his parents! They just transferred him to Heritage High. That was when Ryan was a sophomore.

After a few months at Heritage, Ryan decided to find an easy way to get money so he got a gun and brought it to school to sell it. He didn't think it was "a big deal" but Heritage high expelled him on a "firearms violation."

Ryan Blakeley's parents were outraged and hired a lawyer. The school was forced to pay for a tutor for one year of special education. During that year Ryan watched a lot of TV, talked on the phone to his friends, and asked his mother and father for money to go out on week-ends. They bought him a new red jeep when he got his driver's license just to cheer him up. Finally, their lawyers got Ryan re- admitted to Heritage High.

In the next year Ryan was picked up by the police for breaking and entering. He had started to do drugs and needed more money for his habit – so he stole things. The police brought him up before JUVENILE COURT.

This time the Blakeley's hired the most expensive lawyer in Rutland. He worked hard to provide many character witnesses for Ryan. The judge was swayed by the Blakeley's influence and affluence and the fact that this was Ryan's first offense. Neither previous school incident had made it into court. The judge released Ryan to his parents with the stipulation that he behave and attend the local high school, and if there was a further incident, the parents would have to pay 10,000 dollars.

So, for his senior year Ryan came back to Heritage

High. In a closed school board meeting the members decided that it would be less expensive to re-admit Ryan rather than pay for a private school education. So, Ryan was scheduled into Mrs. Anderson's period 4, Level Two English class – along with Jake, Harry and Jason. She knew about the stink bomb and the gun and was afraid of what he might do next. It didn't take long!

THE PAST JOURNEY

APRIL 10TH - RYAN GOES CRAZY

One week-end, Ryan and his friends from Norwich decided to use a lot more coke than their brains could tolerate. Ryan saw faces, distorted and angry; he couldn't stop being afraid and his mind wouldn't go back to working right.

So, on Monday morning, when Ryan showed up at the Factory, he went "berserk." The principal called the medics and Ryan ended up in s straight jacket in a psyche ward. His parents said it was just a mistake – someone must have slipped Ryan some stuff. They knew he would never take anything because he told them he never touched it. It was all a mistake!

When the psychiatrist suggested Ryan be admitted to the treatment center for addiction to drugs, his parents were outraged. They signed him out of "that crazy place."

For a few months, Ryan stayed out of trouble and came to Mrs. Anderson's class every day. The only problem was he wasn't handing in any work. About half way through the year, Ryan's parents were notified that Ryan wasn't passing English, Math or History.

The parents immediately called a meeting with the principal and teachers to "discuss" Ryan's progress and "get him back on track so he could graduate with his class."

By spring break, Ryan was back on track so his parents decided to take him to the Caribbean at the end of April. While there, he sneaked off and smoked pot and gambled in the casinos but he didn't seem to get into any apparent trouble. What Ryan's parents didn't know was that he had a lot more gambling money than he should have.

By now, Ryan was doing a lot of dealing on the side and he was in a pretty good financial shape. His parents just thought he managed his money real well - that small paycheck he got from working at Burger King.

The dealers, also members of the mafia, had a stash of money in the freezer at the apartment where Ryan made his pickups. Just before Ryan went to the Caribbean, he grabbed about 10,000 dollars from the freezer stash and used it for his gambling.

For a few hours, he felt great - dropping hundred dollar bills on the black jack table. At first he won big! Then he began to lose! But he never gave up because he always thought he would win it back and return the money to the freezer. It never happened. His parents enjoyed a wonderful tour of the island that day. They were so happy they had been able to provide a nice trip for Ryan. After all he was doing so well now!

Ryan came back broke and scared! He heard from another "pusher" that the "dealer" figured out he had taken the money. For a couple of weeks, he hid out. When they found him, they beat him up and told him they'd kill him if he didn't return the money. That was in May – just a few weeks before graduation.

THE PAST JOURNEY

MAY 10ᵀᴴ – PERIOD 5 – LEVEL TWO – ENGLISH CLASS

The kids were already into their "senioritis." They just didn't want to do any work. Mrs. Anderson had handled this sickness before. She had them doing special writing projects in a subject of <u>their</u> choice. They would submit their articles to magazines for publication. Because they were in control of the subject, they loved it. Some were writing about fishing, golf, fashion, alcoholism or any other current social problem.

That morning Mrs. A. was going around the room speaking individually to the kids. She would make suggestions for an edit, or give them samples of a similar article. Sometimes she helped them write a cover letter. Everyone was busy!

Ryan was there with his papers scattered all over the desk pretending to work. Jason was beside him doing the same. Mrs. A could hear the fragmented conversation coming from the back of the room.

"They'll kill me, man.!" "Na ww – no way, man."

"Someone followed me last night." "Na ww – no way."

"This morning same car – right behind me." Ryan confided to his friend. Jason looked frightened. Ryan usually didn't lie to him.

"What are you goin to do?"

Mrs. A. knew by the frightened look on Jason's face that something terrible was going on. The subjects of the other student's papers suddenly lost their importance. She worked her way to the back of the room.

Quietly, she sat down next to Ryan. "Hey, what's happening here, you guys?" she said looking at the papers on the desk but meaning something else.

Terrified, Jason blurted out, "They're goin to kill him."

Hesitating to let more people in, Ryan whispered to his friend to "Shut up."

But Mrs. Anderson knew exactly when to stop asking questions and when not to - so she persisted, "Who's after you, Ryan?"

"I took some money and they found out and they're goin to kill me," Ryan said with complete certitude.

Mrs. A. knew she had to get the rest of the story so she listened carefully as Ryan's story unfolded: "I was goin to the Caribbean, saw the money, I took it, I gambled, I lost it; now, they know and they're goin to kill me."

Ryan <u>never</u> admitted he had dealt drugs – but said he just stopped by the place to pick up a little grass for a friend. Whatever! Now it didn't matter! Soon the whole class, who already knew the situation, joined in the discussion.

"Ryan, you gotta go to your parents and tell them so you can get out of town." One kid offered. Mrs. A. agreed.

"There ain't no other way! These guys will get you!" Another kid offered. Mrs. A. agreed.

Ryan explained further. "Can't tell my parents because the court has this thing that my parents will have to pay if I get in trouble. Shit, I can't do that! If I tell them, <u>they'll</u> kill me."

Everyone laughed nervously.

"Besides I want to graduate. – I'm almost there," Ryan

concluded.

Mrs. A. could see that it was almost time for the bell so she insisted,

"You won't graduate if you're <u>dead.</u> You <u>have</u> to do something, Ryan." The bell cut off the conversation.

Mrs. Anderson knew that the <u>one</u> reason the kids confided in her was because she never broke a confidence. That afternoon she did something she had never done before. She turned in one of her kids. She broke a confidence and saved Ryan's life. The principal paid Ryan's parent's a visit and by nightfall he was on a plane to Kentucky to Aunt Shellie and Uncle Bill. Ryan never did graduate with his class.

BEYOND THE PRESENT

TIMELESSNESS ABOVE THE GRADUATION

Jim continued to teach Mrs. A. "Remember in spirit there is no time. No boundaries. Just timelessness," he continued to prod her.

"You must be concerned about your son. Don't you want to see his future?"

"Of course, but I'm supposed to be there."

When she thought of Robert, her mind moved ahead to his day of graduation from Brown. A pretty dark-haired girl was hugging him. Then, she saw him defending a man in court. How he had grown in stature.

Did he go to Law School? she wondered.

Her mind fast forwarded to a Brownstone on Beacon Hill in Boston. There was Robert coming home to that same pretty dark-haired woman. She was pregnant.

Finally, she saw ROBERT ANDERSON - ATTORNEY AT LAW on the brass name plate on the side of the building. Then, she skipped to an eleventh floor office in that building on Congress Street. She saw her picture on the desk, Robert's desk. Next to her picture was a photo of that same pretty woman and two dark-haired girls.

"They would be my grandchildren? Are you sure I left at the right time?" she asked.

"Yes, the right time!" Jim assured her.

At that moment, she looked down with interest as she saw Eric walk to the podium. She listened to him speak.

JUNE 10ᴛʜ - GRADUATION NIGHT - 7 PM

At 7 0'clock, when the Life star Helicopter flew over the Graduation Ceremony, everyone in the audience looked up. Eric waited a moment while it passed over head. He adjusted the mike the way Mrs. Anderson had shown him. He tried to locate her in the audience but couldn't see her.

Free from her body, Jenny Anderson's spirit was able to look down on the scene. She heard Eric's speech, she saw Leslie Schroeder get her scholarship; she saw Frank eyeing Stacey; she saw Suzy and Justine signal each other: she saw Latisha's disinterested, anxious face; and she noticed that Larry Blaisdell's seat was empty.

BEYOND THE PRESENT

LOOKING BEYOND THE GRADUATION

"What happened to Larry? And to Linda? They helped me!" She asked Jim.

"Think of him - you will know."

When she thought of Larry, she saw him in his truck, speeding to the graduation. He was crying as he drove, his red hair flying in the wind; his sturdy hands gripping the wheel so hard it hurt.

Then she saw Linda Peterson packing up the materials in the ambulance, scrubbing the blood off the floor, piling the dirty linen in a bag, preparing to head home to her cat.

Then, Mrs. A, fast forwarded to Larry and Linda together in a new house over by Emmett's garage — almost where the helicopter put down. There was a little girl with auburn hair and a boy that was a smaller version of Larry — and Linda's cat.

Linda was sitting at the kitchen table listening to the boy read from a school book. He read aloud with confidence and his mother smiled at him when he finished.

Larry joked, "He can read almost as good as me, Linda."

Then to the boy, "You keep it up, Perry and you'll be graduating the top of your class." The boy smiled at his dad.

Jim motioned to Mrs. A. to listen to the orchestra

as they were about to begin.

JUNE 10ᴛʜ - GRADUATION NIGHT - 7:30 PM

Ken Stanton conducted the musical version of Beethoven's Ode to Joy. Then, he nodded to Alex at the back of the stage. The program read "A Special Musical Tribute to Jim Bartlett ….. Performed by Alex Brady."

Alex tuned his guitar, came forward and nodded to Ken Stanton to let him know he was ready. For a moment he looked skyward indicating "this is for you Jim." The orchestra began to play. As Alex started to sing Billy Joel's "James", the audience grew silent.

"James, we were always friends – from our childhood days – and we made our plans - And we had to go our separate ways   "

The class of 2007 began to blur in the diminishing sunlight. The colors in the blue and white gown became less intense, as faces were shadowed, less prominent. The red roses began to look purple. Sunlight and shadows stood still. No one moved.

"James, do you like your life – can you find release? ——-Will you ever change? When will you write your masterpiece? "

Alex continued with the orchestra behind him. Jim's mother, who was sitting alone in the front row, tensed as she tried to squeeze back the tears. Chet Bartlett was not there. He was on the road and besides he couldn't understand the importance of coming just to hear a kid sing a song.

"James--- You were well behaved   You were so relied upon. Everybody knows how hard you tried – Look

what a job you've done —carrying the weight of family pride."

Anita Bartlett took out her handkerchief from her purse and wiped the tears from her face. She missed her son every day but especially today. Just to hear his name was painful. The song went on:

"James   will you always say someone's else's dream of who you are?------ Do what's good for you - or you're not good for anybody-----James   James!"

From up above, Jim Bartlett and Jenny Anderson could hear the music. She saw her empty seat beside Mrs. Bartlett. She knew she should be there to console her, but couldn't go there. Then, somehow it was alright. Jim, who was with her held her essence within his, and reassured her by his peaceful presence.

No sound. Just the song. And the cry of a baby.

Kurt sat with the graduates and kept a tearless face. His eyes straight ahead but inside he hid a pain that cut deeper than his stoic public face would dare betray. Jenny Anderson and Jim Bartlett saw inside Kurt's soul — a white light as hard as tempered steel, as soft as moonlight. A flash of memory came to Jim. Mrs. A. supported him with her being as they both turned their thoughts to Kurt.

BEYOND THE PRESENT

LOOKING BEYOND THE GRADUATION

They saw Kurt's future fast forwarded. First, all

his art work being bought by Mrs. Abbott – on display at the Heritage library.

Then, they watched him at The Cleveland School of Art – his master's program there and the room on the third floor where his fiery work was displayed. The first honors and showings and the acclaim! So much acclaim!

Then they recognized his work at the Metropolitan Museum of Art in New York and the National Gallery in Washington. They saw him working and teaching in his own studio in Rutland during the summer months – and alone in his Manhattan apartment in winter. Jim saw his awards displayed on the wall,

Jim Bartlett and Jenny Anderson followed him as he was commissioned to do more significant works. They watched his triumphant return to Heritage on a day named specifically for him. His quiet, meaningful visit with an old widow, now living alone – Anita Bartlett.

Finally, they saw him in his later years living with another artist in Tuscany, Italy. Then, his death publicized all over the world. Renowned artist dies!

Time on earth would end there for Kurt but Jim knew that on that day Kurt would rejoin him – seeing their reunion brought great joy to him.

JUNE 10ᵀᴴ - GRADUATION NIGHT - 7:45 PM

Mrs. Anderson and Jim continued to watch from this new place as the Graduation proceeded. Finally, diplomas were delivered to anxious hands. Larry made a late entry and Mr. McManus called his name at the end rather than the beginning. Everyone laughed and cheered.

Then, they saw Josh lumbering across the stage, vehemently pumping Mr. Mc Manus's hand. "Th-thank You! Th-thank you!" More cheers from the seniors.

And after the last diploma, the hats were tossed in the air. All hats returned to the ground except Kurt's and Larry's – somehow they got lost but no one was surprised.

Kurt forgot about his misplaced hat when he went to greet Jim's mother. Larry forgot about his as he hurried to find Mr. McManus to explain why he was late and what had happened to Mrs. A.

Mrs. A. and Jim pulled back from the scene. Two graduation hats floated up like helium balloons. No one noticed. Then, Billy looked up saying, "Hats go way high, grampy."

His grandfather never looked up but just agreed with the child, "Yes, Billy Hats Go high."

THE BEGINNING OF A NEW LIFE
GRADUATION DAY ENDED AT 8 PM

About the Author

Christine A. Adams

Christine A. Adams, M.A., has been writing about issues of addiction, relationships, spirituality, and education for over 35 years. She has over 3,000,000 separate books and pamphlets in print with works published in 54 countries translated into many languages. Christine, an English teacher, was also formerly trained as an addiction counselor in 1986. However, most of her writing parallels her life experiences. Her early writings were about the alcoholic marriage, adult children of alcoholics, teen alcoholism, and sexual addiction. Then came books about spirituality, relationships, grief therapy and education.

In addition, she has produced four very popular Elf Help children's books: Happy To Be Me, Learning To Be A Good Friend, Worry, Worry, Go Away, and God Made Us One By One. One of her best-known recovery books is the adult Elf Help gift book, One Day At A Time Therapy which is still selling in places like Taiwan, China, South Korea, Portugal, the Netherlands, Austria, Sweden, Indonesia, and Brazil.

Among her other books are: <u>Seasons: Spiritual Meditations for Winter, Spring, Summer, and Fall</u>; <u>Let Go, Let God</u>; <u>Teacher of God</u>; <u>Holy Relationships</u>; and <u>ABC's of Grief: A Handbook For Survivors</u>. She has also written a fictional narrative, inspired by her years of teaching, titled <u>The School Factory</u>, as well as a romantic novel named <u>September Love</u>. Additionally, she has authored four out of the five titles in the <u>Spiritual Way of Life</u> series, which encompass Joy, Peace, Love, Acceptance, and Gratitude.

Visit her at <u>www.christineaadams.com</u> or <u>www.hanleyadamspublishing.com</u>   to find all her books.

Also by Christine A. Adams

Peace: A Spiritual Way of Life

Love: A Spiritual Way of Life

Acceptance: A Spiritual Way of Life

Gratitude: A Spiritual Way of Life

Seasons: Spiritual Meditations For Winter, Spring, Summer, and Fall

Spirituality: A Life Force

ABC's of Grief – A Handbook for Survivors

Let Go and Let God

Teacher of God

Holy Relationships

Living in Love

September Love

Claiming Your Own Life

School Factory

Love, Infidelity, and Sexual Addiction

Gratitude Therapy

One Day At A Time

Learning To Be A Good Friend

Happy To Be Me

Worry, Worry, Go Away

God Made Us One By One